Also from Indigo Sea Press
by Marietta Rodgers

The Bill

indigoseapress.com

Looney Bin Incorporated

By

Marietta Rodgers

Deep Indigo Books
Published by Indigo Sea Press
Winston-Salem

Deep Indigo Books
Indigo Sea Press
302 Ricks Drive
Winston-Salem, NC 27103

First Deep Indigo Books edition published
January, 2016
Deep Indigo Books, Moon Sailor and all production design are trademarks of Indigo Sea Press, used under license.

For information regarding bulk purchases of this book, digital purchase and special discounts, please contact the publisher at indigoseapress.com

Cover design by Pan Morelli

Manufactured in the United States of America
ISBN 978-1-63066-355-1

Special thanks to Mike Simpson and the folks at Indigo Sea Press for working tiresomely over my novel & giving me a chance to show my work to the world.

To my roses Madison and Liam.

To Jeff, Mary & Kaitlyn, you guys are wonderful.

In loving memory of Harriet Douglas for teaching me, "it's in front of the at" something that has always stayed with me.

Chapter 1

"You are a pessimist; that's what you are," Potbelly said.

"I am not a pessimist; I am an absurdist and there is a big difference," Crazy Bob said.

"I don't see a difference," Potbelly said.

"I simply embrace the philosophy that things happen; and when they do, I'm either happy or sad, depending on the nature of the thing. The very fact that if I won the lottery, I would be quite happy about it proves I'm not a pessimist," Crazy Bob said.

"That's not a good example. You don't play the lottery," Potbelly said.

"I don't play the lottery because that would require the hope that you could win, and I reject hope," Crazy Bob said.

"But if you reject hope, doesn't that automatically make you a pessimist?" Potbelly asked.

"The rejection of hope has nothing to do with despair since I believe that they are not opposites," Crazy Bob said.

"Maybe you are a nihilist then," Drake said.

"Oh, hang you both! I don't want to talk about *ists* or *isms* anymore," Potbelly said.

Potbelly sat in his seat pouting. Despite his name, he didn't have a Potbelly; he was very thin. If he had a name derived from his physique, he would probably be called String Bean or some other synonym. His name came from the fact that he had a fascination with pot-bellied pigs. He used to own three of them before he came to the looney bin.

Crazy Bob could see that he had pushed his joke a little too far and Potbelly would probably pout for the rest of the day so he asked him about his favorite subject.

"What is the life expectancy of a pot-bellied pig?" Crazy Bob asked.

Crazy Bob knew the answer already because in the thirty-five years that they had been together in the looney bin, Potbelly had told him everything he knew about pot-bellied pigs. Drake had been there twenty-five years. They knew as much about pot-bellied pigs as Potbelly. They were all experts on the subject.

Potbelly immediately perked up.

"Well, if you take really good care of your pig and watch its diet, they can have a life expectancy of ten to fifteen years. It may be longer these days, what with all the new scientific advancements and all," Potbelly said.

"What scientific advancements?" Drake asked.

"I don't know; the usual kind, I guess. I've been asking Nurse Lovington to get me some books about pot-bellied pigs, but she keeps saying there are none. She says I must be the only person interested in them. She thinks maybe I should write a book about them," Potbelly said.

"That's probably a good idea, since there are no books about pot-bellied pigs. You could write one in case someone else was interested but couldn't find any information about them," Crazy Bob said.

"Maybe you should ask some of the younger patients, like Joseph or Abram; they might know more about all the new developments on pot-bellied pigs," Drake said.

"I have, but no one has any newer information, especially Joseph; you can't get two words out of him. So maybe they haven't advanced all that much," Potbelly said.

"I'll let you know all about them when I get out of here the day after tomorrow," Crazy Bob said.

They watched as Lester walked into the dayroom. He always walked hunched over forward and very slowly as if he were trying to sneak up on you. He thinks he works for the CIA and is currently undercover. In reality he never worked for the CIA; he was a copier repairman. On the way over to their table, he accidentally bumped into Joseph at the foosball table.

"I'm sorry, Joseph; I didn't see you there," Lester said.

No one ever saw Joseph there because the problem with Joseph was that he was invisible. He wasn't invisible in the sense that no one listened to him or he was always ignored; he was invisible in the sense that he literally couldn't be seen.

Lester surveyed the group of misfits.

Crazy Bob was wearing a red flannel shirt. He always wore flannel, even in the summer time. His bifocals were thick and black; that made him look like Buddy Holly. Well, that is if Buddy Holly would have lived long enough to become bald like Crazy Bob was. Crazy Bob, except for a little hair on the sides, was as bald as a baby's butt.

Drake, unlike Crazy Bob, had a head full of curly red hair. His full name was Drake Shannon, and his grandparents had come to America from Cork, Ireland. They had dreams of making it big in America; they never did, but they didn't give up hope that their four children would. None of their children ever really made it in America either; they just got by. Out of all four children, only one of them had a child; and that child was Drake. The grandparents lived long enough to see Drake committed to the looney bin; and then they both died, brokenhearted and regretting that they had ever left their homeland.

Potbelly still had hair as well, although he had a receding hairline; he was somewhere in between Crazy Bob and Drake on the hair spectrum. Potbelly had a pug nose, which was fitting since he liked pigs so much.

"What are you guys doing?" Lester asked.

"We are waiting," Drake said.

"Waiting for what?" Lester asked.

"Waiting for Godot," Crazy Bob said.

Crazy Bob winked at Drake.

"Waiting for what?" Lester asked.

"Not *what* but *who*," Drake said.

"Is he a new patient?" Lester asked

Potbelly didn't get the joke; he still thought they were talking about pot-bellied pigs.

"I never had a pot-bellied pig named Godot. I had one named Francis, one named Big Pig and the other Priscilla," Potbelly said.

"Yes, he is a new patient," Crazy Bob said.

"What's going on?" Drake asked.

"Did you hear that Dr. Olive and Dr. Boyd had to drag Abram away from the soda machine and give him a sedative?" Lester asked.

"Why did they have to drag him away and give him a sedative?" Crazy Bob asked.

"He was highly agitated. He wanted a drink, but the drink machine would not take his nickel. It took his two quarters but refused to take his nickel," Lester said.

"Why did the machine refuse his nickel? What does it have against nickels?" Potbelly asked.

"It was a Canadian nickel so the machine wouldn't accept it," Lester said.

"So it doesn't have anything against nickels, it has something against Canada," Drake said.

"I went to Canada once," Potbelly said.

"Did they take your nickels?" Drake asked.

"No, they did not take my nickels, nor my dimes, pennies,

quarters or dollar bills. In fact, I had to exchange all my money into Canadian money," Potbelly said.

"Ah, so there is a mutual dislike of the other's money, it seems," Drake said.

"Yes, it's been that way ever since some of the Northern colonies of Canada allied with the British during the Revolutionary War. There are some leftover hostilities; and as a result, neither side will touch the other's money. I know these things; I was a professor at Harvard," Crazy Bob said.

"I don't know about any of that; I just know he didn't get his drink," Lester said.

"Well, why should he expect to get a drink? The machine was just doing its patriotic duty," Crazy Bob said.

"What did you buy in Canada, Potbelly?" Drake asked.

"I bought a shirt and a pair of socks," Potbelly said.

"You bought a shirt and a pair of socks? We have those here," Crazy Bob said.

"Yes, but these were a Canadian shirt and socks which is why I had to pay more for them," Potbelly said.

"Why would you drive all the way to Canada to pay more for a shirt and a pair of socks?" Drake asked.

"I didn't drive to Canada just to get a shirt and a pair of socks. I was on vacation, and I happened to need a shirt and a pair of socks," Potbelly said.

"Was there anything special about the shirt and socks?" Crazy Bob asked.

"No, they were just your regular shirt and socks," Potbelly said.

"I still don't get why you paid more for them," Crazy Bob asked.

"I don't really get it myself; I just know I had to pay more," Potbelly said.

"No wonder the drink machine refused to take the nickel. I wouldn't either if a country is going to go around charging more for the same stuff everybody else has," Drake said.

"They got other stuff too, like maple syrup," Potbelly said.

"We have maple syrup here also," Crazy Bob said.

Potbelly shrugged.

"I don't know about shirts, socks or maple syrup; but the machine didn't take Abram's nickel," Lester said.

"I think we have firmly established that fact already, Lester," Crazy Bob said.

4

"It's probably a secret Canadian plot to take over all the drink machines in the United States. You know not a lot of people know this; but during the time we had a Cold War with the former Soviet Union, we also had a Cold War with Canada," Lester said.

"We had a Cold War with Canada?" Crazy Bob repeated in disbelief.

"Was it like the one with Russia?" Potbelly asked.

"No, it was a warmer war. Canada is not as cold as Russia. So we referred to it as a Luke Warm War," Lester said.

"Who won the war?" Drake asked.

"No one; it was a tie," Lester said.

"That's fascinating," Crazy Bob said.

Nurse Lovington walked in carrying a tray of medication.

"I believe it's time for our medication," Drake said.

"I wonder if any of the medication comes from Canada," Potbelly said.

"We can ask; and if any of it does, I think we should refuse to take it," Drake said.

"Yes, let's win the Cold War against Canada," Potbelly said.

"Well, then it's settled. I'm getting out of here the day after tomorrow anyway. We will all refuse to take our medication," Crazy Bob said.

"You mean only the medication that comes from Canada?" Potbelly asked.

"No, you can't trust those Canadians and their pharmaceutical drugs. No doubt some of them are operating in the United States, masquerading as American drug companies," Lester said.

"Okay then, it's agreed: no drugs of any kind," Crazy Bob said.

Chapter 2

"Now, Robert, I'd like for you to tell me more about the bugs in your room," Dr. Boyd said.

Dr. Boyd was a handsome middle-aged man who came from a wealthy family. He had lived with his mother until he was thirty-two years old before finally taking an apartment. On his first night alone, he called his mother and cried. He wanted to come home; he didn't like being alone. So the next day he moved back in with his mother and lived with her until her death last year. He inherited all of her money; and now at the age of forty, he was the most eligible bachelor in the city.

"I would like something to be done about the stink bugs in my room. The room is full of them; they crawl over me when I'm sleeping. They are a nuisance, and they stink up my room," Crazy Bob said.

"Have you been killing them?" Dr. Boyd asked.

"Not a single one," Crazy Bob said.

"Well, then your room shouldn't stink," Dr. Boyd said.

"What do you mean? My room is full of stink bugs; so, therefore, by default, my room is going to stink," Crazy Bob said.

"They only stink when you kill them or swat at them," Dr. Boyd said.

"What's that?" Crazy Bob asked.

"The stink bug has a stink gland that secretes an odor when you injure or kill them," Dr. Boyd said.

"So you mean it farts when it feels threatened?" Crazy Bob asked.

"Something like that," Dr. Boyd said.

"Well, I'll be. Come to think of it, I do the same thing. You know they should just be called fart bugs then," Crazy Bob said.

"Nurse Lovington said she checked your room and couldn't find a single one," Dr. Boyd said.

"Nurse Lovington can't find any books about pot-bellied pigs either so I wouldn't expect her to be able to find a fart bug," Crazy Bob said.

"Do you think they might not be real, Robert?" Dr. Boyd asked.

"Well, of course they are real. They crawl all over me while I'm asleep. I am constantly scratching all night," Crazy Bob said.

Crazy Bob lifted his flannel shirt up to reveal patches of red skin.

"See, Doc; look at this. My skin is raw from all the scratching," Crazy Bob said.

"I see," Dr. Boyd said.

"At least I won't have to worry about fart bugs when I get out of here the day before Monday," Crazy Bob said.

Dr. Boyd scribbled something down on his note pad.

Crazy Bob picked up the snow globe on his desk and shook it. He watched as all the snow went up into the air and landed on a group of kids ice skating. He put the snow globe back down and waited.

Dr. Boyd watched him over the rim of his glasses. He had been Robert's doctor for the past ten years, before that he had Dr. Beaumont and before that he had Dr. Wells and before that there was Dr. Frisch. Robert had been here thirty-five years, and each doctor had passed along their notes about him to the next doctor. There was enough information on Robert Ellsworth to fill up a library.

"I understand you have stopped taking your medication," Dr. Boyd said.

"Yes, I have. I believe it is my duty as a citizen of this country," Crazy Bob said.

"What does being a citizen of this country have to do with taking your medication?" Dr. Boyd asked.

"I don't want to take foreign medications," Crazy Bob said.

"What do you mean by 'foreign'?" Dr. Boyd asked.

"You know, not made in the USA," Crazy Bob said.

"None of your medications are foreign; the companies that make them are all based here in the United States," Dr. Boyd said.

"Yes, but are all the ingredients that are used to make the pills made in the United States?" Crazy Bob asked. "Lester says that some of them are probably fronts for Canadian drug companies."

"What does it matter where they come from? What matters is that you take them," Dr. Boyd said.

"How can you say that? Didn't you fight in Vietnam?" Crazy Bob asked.

"No, I didn't fight in Vietnam," Dr. Boyd said.

"Well, neither did I," Crazy Bob said.

"I still fail to see the connection here," Dr. Boyd said.

"The connection is that I just don't believe it is right for a soldier to fight in Vietnam while I run around taking foreign medications. It's a disservice to our veterans," Crazy Bob said.

"I see. Have you been seeing your wife again?" Dr. Boyd asked.

"No, but I did have a dream about her," Crazy Bob said.

"Can you tell me about the dream?" Dr. Boyd asked.

"We were sitting in a yellow room, much like this one. Why is your office painted yellow?" Crazy Bob asked.

"I find it comforting. How do you feel about yellow?" Dr. Boyd asked.

"I find yellow a little effeminate; I prefer a more masculine color like red or blue," Crazy Bob said.

Dr. Boyd ignored the slight on his masculinity.

"Do you feel any association with your wife and the color yellow?" Dr. Boyd asked.

"Yes, she painted our living room yellow," Crazy Bob said.

"What happened in the dream?" Dr. Boyd asked.

"She was sitting in the armchair knitting me a sweater. I was on the couch watching television. The news was on, and there was a report about a man who had stabbed his wife to death. It was gruesome; he stabbed her over a hundred times," Crazy Bob said.

"How did that make you feel?" Dr. Boyd asked.

"It made me feel cold. I started to shiver uncontrollably. That's when my wife held up the sweater and said it was finished. I took the sweater and put it on. It was the warmest sweater I've ever worn. I didn't feel cold anymore, and that's how the dream ended," Crazy Bob said.

"What color was the sweater?" Dr. Boyd asked.

"It was a vibrant blue. It reminded me of the water in the Bahamas where my wife and I took our honeymoon. The water there was warm and felt good on my skin. When I put the sweater on, it enveloped me in that same kind of warmth," Crazy Bob said.

Dr. Boyd scribbled something else down in his notes.

"Can I see what you are writing?" Crazy Bob asked.

This caught Dr. Boyd off guard.

"Why do you want to see what I've written?" Dr. Boyd asked.

"I've come in here for the past thirty-five years and shot the breeze with every doctor, including you; and each one of you periodically writes stuff down as I'm talking. I'd like to know what it is that I am saying that prompts you to have to write it down. I didn't think I was saying anything that profound, but I must be if you feel the urge to write it down," Crazy Bob said.

"It's so I won't forget what we've discussed," Dr. Boyd said.

"Well, if all doctors do that, then you must have thirty-five years' worth of conversations I've had in here," Crazy Bob said.

"Yes, I keep my files here in the office; the files from your previous doctors are in the file room," Dr. Boyd said.

"So did you write down stuff about fart bugs and sweaters that look and feel like the big blue water from the Bahamas?" Crazy Bob asked.

"Yes, that's the gist of it," Dr. Boyd said.

Crazy Bob chuckled and said, "Well, I'll be damned."

"I really want you to take your medications. How are you going to control your delusions?" Dr. Boyd asked.

"What delusions?" Crazy Bob asked.

"The delusions about your wife and that there are stink bugs in your room, just to name a few," Dr. Boyd said.

"They aren't delusions; they are real. I know what's real and what isn't. You and I are real. This desk is real; that snow globe is real. What isn't real is ghosts, Frankenstein, unicorns and disco," Crazy Bob said.

"Disco is real," Dr. Boyd said.

"Where have you been, Doc? Disco is dead," Crazy Bob said.

"I see; well, I guess you're right," Dr. Boyd said.

Dr. Boyd took a moment to jot something down.

"How come you're not married, Dr. Boyd?" Crazy Bob asked.

Dr. Boyd, a little startled by the question, said, "I just haven't met the right person yet."

"You haven't met the right guy," Crazy Bob said.

"Um, yes…I mean no. I'm not gay; I like women," Dr. Boyd said.

"Doc, I am a man of science, a man of observation. All the facts point to you being as gay as a Christmas ham. Now don't be offended; no one cares that you're gay, but I think it's time that you admitted it to yourself," Crazy Bob said.

"I see and what are the facts? What have you observed?" Dr. Boyd asked.

"You carry a purse," Crazy Bob said.

"I don't carry a purse," Dr. Boyd said.

Crazy Bob pointed to the bag hanging up on the coat rack.

"I see it hanging right there," Crazy Bob said.

"That's not a purse; it's a messenger bag," Dr. Boyd said.

"And do you carry any messages in that bag?" Crazy Bob asked.

9

"I carry my laptop in it," Dr. Boyd said.

"You have a messenger bag, but you don't carry any messages in it. You say you carry your lap top in it, but your lap top is sitting right in front of you," Crazy Bob said.

"I'm not carrying my laptop right now; I'm using it," Dr. Boyd said.

"So you have a bag hanging on your coat rack with neither a laptop nor messages in it?" Crazy Bob asked.

"Yes, but—"

Crazy Bob interrupted, "So you admit that you are gay."

"Yes...I mean no," Dr. Boyd said, flustered.

"Doc, I think you might be the one suffering from delusions. You might need my medication more than me," Crazy Bob said.

He looked at the time and said, "I believe our time is up."

Dr. Boyd, who was still flustered and tongue-tied, said nothing.

Crazy Bob turned to leave and noticed Dr. Boyd's belt.

"You know you shouldn't wear a black belt and carry a brown bag. If you want to be gay, you'll have to learn these things."

Chapter 3

Crazy Bob was curious and wanted to get in the file room to see what the other doctors had written about him. The file room was always locked, but Crazy Bob knew where Dr. Boyd kept his key. He kept it underneath his snow globe, which Crazy Bob picked up to give it a shake every time he was in the office.

He stood in the hallway in front of the file room and checked to make sure no one was around before trying the key. The key required a few jiggles before it gave way. Crazy Bob pushed the door to the file room open. He closed the door and turned on the light. All the shelves were filled with boxes; in fact, every shelf was full, and there were some boxes on the floor.

Crazy Bob walked around the room, looking at each box. To his surprise, each and every box was labeled "Robert Ellsworth" with the year on it. It was incredible: a whole file room filled with nothing but his life. There were no other patients' files in here, not even Potbelly's, who had also been there thirty-five years or Drake, who had been there twenty-five years.

They probably have their own in an offsite storage facility, Crazy Bob thought.

Twenty-five years of his life were here. The other ten were locked away in the file cabinet in Dr. Boyd's office, but he didn't know where Dr. Boyd kept the key for those. So he would have to be content with this room and he was. He was more than content; he was ecstatic. He felt like he did the same day he was floating on his back in the ocean when he was on his honeymoon with his wife. He was weightless, unburdened and happy.

He started with the box from his first year here. His doctor at that time was Dr. Frisch. Dr. Frisch only worked there one year and left. It was his first position right out of college, and the strain of having a patient like Crazy Bob was too much for him. He ran away to a remote island in the Caribbean and was never heard from again. Crazy Bob remembered that he had trouble remembering his name and always called him Dr. Fish.

He pulled out a file and looked through it. The file had no handwritten notes or forms; in fact, it didn't have any writing in it at all, only pictures that Dr. Frisch had drawn.

One of the pictures was of Crazy Bob in a chair, and Dr. Frisch was hanging from his ceiling fan with a noose around his neck.

He pulled out another picture. It was of Crazy Bob sitting in his office, and Dr. Frisch had a gun to his head. All the pictures were like this; each one showed Crazy Bob in his office and Dr. Frisch attempting to kill himself by one method or the other.

Interesting. All the while he was treating me, he was really depressed himself. I guess even doctors have problems, he thought, remembering Dr. Boyd's struggle with his sexuality.

This was not the case at all, though; Dr. Frisch wasn't depressed, at least not until he started working at the looney bin. He just found his sessions with Crazy Bob frustrating because he could never get anything sensible out of the man, so he drew pictures to pass the time.

For the next eight years or so, he had Dr. Wells. Dr. Wells had drawn no pictures at all, but he had written quite extensively. Crazy Bob noticed that his boxes were labeled by month rather than by year. Dr. Wells had three times as many boxes as all the other doctors.

Crazy Bob pulled out a sheet of paper and began to read.

"Judy had lusted after Brad for over ten years now, and there he stood at her door. Judy had on a tank top with a low neckline and cut-off jean shorts. Her cleavage was glistening because the air conditioner had been broken for two days now, but Brad was about to fix that problem. In fact, he was about to fix all of her problems. He asked her if she were hot, and she replied that she was; she was hot for him. He touched the swell of her breast and…"

What the hell is this? Who are Judy and Brad? Crazy Bob wondered.

All the other files were filled with the same kind of stuff. They were full of Judy and Brad meeting each other in some contrived scenario, where Judy's cleavage was glistening with sweat, and her breasts were being fondled. It was nothing but erotic fiction. The boxes were full of papers, and yet not one word of it was about him.

It looks like Dr. Wells had problems too, only he was addicted to smut. I guess if you have to be an addict of any kind, that's the best one to be, he thought.

The remaining years that were in the file room were with Dr. Beaumont.

He looked through one box with Dr. Beaumont and stuffed all the files back in there angrily. They were all written in French. Crazy

Bob remembered now that Dr. Beaumont was from Toulouse, France, and never spoke a word of English. Crazy Bob would come into his office and speak for an hour, and Dr. Beaumont would write things down and sometimes respond to him in French; and Crazy Bob never understood a word he was saying.

Sometimes he would just nod along and pretend he understood, and sometimes he would shrug his shoulders. Dr. Beaumont would smile at him and continue writing. Crazy Bob didn't mind at the time that he couldn't understand him because he thought the sound of his French was very pleasant, and he always felt better after leaving his office; but now he regretted not being able to understand him because he wanted to read about himself.

I cannot believe it. I have given thirty-five years, the best years of my life, to a place; and there's nothing, not one word written about me. Dr. Boyd writes things down, but it's probably nothing useful like the others, he thought.

Then Crazy Bob had an epiphany, one of Crazy Bob's more optimistic epiphanies.

I know who I am and what I've done. I don't need anyone else's opinions. I can write it down and formulate my own opinions.

He left the room that was dedicated solely to him. The fact that it didn't contain any information about him no longer troubled him. After all, he was a scientific man. His eyes were like microscopes, and his brain was like a computer; he could observe the world and his place in it for himself.

Chapter 4

Crazy Bob was sitting at his usual table in his usual chair with his usual friends in the dayroom. When you've spent thirty-five years in the looney bin, everything is usual. The dayroom was yellow too, the same color as Dr. Boyd's office.

Everyone must find that damn color comforting but me, Crazy Bob thought.

He was reading a book. He was always reading a book. The rest of the time when he was not reading a book, he was crazy.

Those were his only hobbies.

"What book are you reading?" Drake asked.

"It's not a book; it's an epic poem called *Inferno* by Dante Alighieri. I taught it to my students at Yale in my early European masterpieces class," Crazy Bob said.

"That must be the longest poem ever written. What's it about?" Potbelly asked.

"What isn't it about?" Crazy Bob said.

"I asked what it was about. How will I know if I want to read it or not if I only know what it's not about?" Potbelly asked.

"I meant it has everything: pride, lust, greed, envy, you name it. The main character takes a tour through hell," Crazy Bob said.

"Why would you want to take a tour through hell?" Drake asked.

"Curiosity," Crazy Bob said.

"You said he was taking a tour. Was he on vacation?" Potbelly asked.

"Not quite, but he did have a tour guide named Virgil," Crazy Bob said.

"You mean that guy who's in solitary confinement in Ward B?" Potbelly asked.

"No, that is not the guy. Virgil, the great poet and writer," Crazy Bob said.

"How do you know that Virgil in solitary isn't a better writer than this Virgil? You can't know because he has been here only six months and has spent all six in solitary confinement," Drake said.

"A fair point; when he gets out of solitary confinement, we shall ask to see his writing so we can compare them both to see who is the better writer," Crazy Bob said.

"How do the pride, lust and greed that you mentioned come into the story?" Drake asked.

"Virgil takes him through the nine levels of hell. The first level is limbo where Virgil lives," Crazy Bob said.

"They play limbo in hell?" Potbelly asked.

"They have to play for all eternity," Crazy Bob said.

"That's really bad!" Drake said.

"What are the other levels?" Potbelly asked.

"The levels are lust, gluttony, greed, wrath, heresy, violence, fraud and treachery," Crazy Bob said.

"Aren't gluttony and greed synonyms of each other?" Drake asked.

"So are wrath and violence," Potbelly said.

"I don't see your point," Crazy Bob said.

"It's really semantics, isn't it? I mean what is the real difference between being gluttonous and being greedy? Couldn't you combine some of these levels?" Drake asked.

"I think it's because people who are greedy don't like to be accused of being gluttonous and vice versa," Crazy Bob said.

"But what is the difference, though?" Drake asked.

"It's semantics just like you said," Crazy Bob said.

"I think when I die, I will go to the lust level for sure," Drake laughed.

"I will probably end up in level one, even though I also quality for three, four and six," Crazy Bob said.

"I think I qualify for all of them," Potbelly said.

"You only get to go to one, so I guess you get placed in the one that you were the worst," Crazy Bob said.

"I must be the worst at semantics," Drake said.

"There is not a level for semantics, though; that is just poor education, and you're not faulted for poor education," Crazy Bob said.

"As long as I don't have to do the limbo, I don't care which of the others they put me in," Potbelly said.

"Did Dante see anyone he knew down there?" Drake asked.

"Yeah, lots," Crazy Bob said.

"How big is hell?" Drake asked.

"Very big, bigger than you can possibly imagine," Crazy Bob said.

"How does he run into so many people he knows if it's so big? I never even ran into one person I knew when I went anywhere," Potbelly said.

15

"They saw him because being the only living person among the dead, you kind of stand out," Crazy Bob said.

"What kinds of conversations did they have?" Drake asked.

"You know, small talk," Crazy Bob said.

"I guess it's rude to ask how someone's doing in hell," Potbelly said.

"Yes, that would be very rude," Crazy Bob said.

"Did they see Satan?" Drake asked.

"Yes, he is in the last circle. He has three faces," Crazy Bob said.

"I believe the expression is two-faced; you added an extra face," Drake said.

"No, I mean he literally has three faces, and each face is gnawing on a betrayer. They are Judas, Brutus and Cassius," Crazy Bob said.

"Why did he pick those three? Why not Hitler, Stalin and Pol Pot or even Virgil from solitary confinement, for that matter," Potbelly said.

"Why would Satan be gnawing on Virgil from solitary confinement? Did he betray someone?" Crazy Bob asked.

"For all we know, he may have; and that's how he ended up in solitary confinement. We will have to find out when he gets out. If he has, I will tell him that Satan is going to gnaw on him for all eternity," Potbelly said.

"He doesn't actually eat them; he just gnaws on them?" Drake asked.

"Yeah, kind of like you do with beef jerky. You never really eat that stuff; it's too hard," Crazy Bob said.

"Did Dante enjoy his tour through hell?" Potbelly asked.

"It doesn't say; I like to think he did, though," Crazy Bob said.

"What about Virgil; did Dante leave him a big tip?" Drake asked.

"I don't think Dante gave him any money," Crazy Bob said.

"What a cheap bastard. I mean if someone gave me a tour through hell, I'd give them a little something for their time," Potbelly said.

"Well, Dante was Italian and they are known for their passion and their food. They are not known to be big tippers," Crazy Bob said.

"I guess he doesn't need money if he is such a great writer. He's probably making money hand over fist," Drake said.

"I don't think so because he's dead. I think after you die, you stop earning royalties," Crazy Bob said.

"I'm definitely not going to read this book. I don't like the ending," Potbelly said.

"I don't like the ending either; that's why I've never read the book all the way through," Crazy Bob said.

"I prefer books on tape anyway," Potbelly said.

"How do you read a tape?" Crazy Bob asked.

"You don't read it; you listen to it," Potbelly said.

"I've never tried to listen to tape; it's too sticky," Crazy Bob said.

"Well, you should try it sometime," Potbelly said.

"I didn't get a chance to tell you guys, but I got into the file room and read some of my old files," Crazy Bob said.

"Did you see any of my files in there?" Drake asked.

"No, there were no one else's files in there but mine," Crazy Bob said.

"How many boxes were in there?" Drake asked.

"Hundreds, probably," Crazy Bob said.

"There were hundreds of boxes, and they were all about you?" Potbelly asked.

"Not a one," Crazy Bob said.

"I'm confused," Drake said.

"There were hundreds of boxes in the file room; they each had my name on it and the year, but there was nothing about me in them. There were drawings and stuff about Brad and Judy and French words," Crazy Bob said.

"Who are Brad and Judy?" Drake asked.

"I don't know; I think Dr. Wells liked to write erotic fiction because it's all about Brad wanting to fix something of Judy's and touching her breasts," Crazy Bob said.

"I would like to read one of my files," Drake said.

"I'd like to read Brad and Judy's files," Potbelly said.

"I already returned the key I stole; I put it back underneath Dr. Boyd's snow globe," Crazy Bob said.

"He keeps the key underneath his snow globe and not in his purse?" Potbelly asked.

"No, it's a messenger bag," Crazy Bob said.

"What kind of messages? Are they top secret war dispatches?" Drake asked.

"No. He doesn't have any written messages; he keeps his laptop in it so all the messages are probably on the lap top," Crazy Bob said.

"I wish I had a purse," Potbelly said.

17

"Messenger bag," Crazy Bob corrected.

"I wish I had a messenger bag," Potbelly said.

"You can't get one," Crazy Bob said.

"Why not?" Potbelly asked.

Potbelly looked really anxious; Crazy Bob was afraid he was going to start obsessing over messenger bags now, and they'd never hear the end of it. He needed to nip this in the bud.

"Because you're not a gay man who carries a lap top with messages," Crazy Bob said.

"Oh, right," Potbelly said.

"I'd like to read my files; where do you think they are?" Drake asked.

"I guess they would be in Dr. Olive's office," Crazy Bob said.

"I don't know where he keeps his keys, though," Drake said.

"He keeps his keys in his desk drawer. I saw them one time when he was taking out a note pad," Potbelly said.

"How can I get them out of his desk drawer?" Drake asked.

"We need to create a diversion," Crazy Bob said.

"How about we start a riot like we did in '95, '96 and '04," Potbelly said.

"Not like in '96, though; that one patient lost an eye. What was his name?" Crazy Bob asked.

"His name was Cyclops," Potbelly said.

"No, I mean what was his name before he lost the eye?" Crazy Bob asked.

"That was his name," Potbelly said.

"Oh yeah, good name; his mother must have known he'd lose an eye one day," Crazy Bob said.

"Okay, let's start a riot then," Drake said.

"Well, I don't want to kill anyone; that's a little too drastic. I know, Potbelly and I will start fighting while Drake sneaks into Dr. Olive's office," Crazy Bob said.

"We'll start tomorrow; we need to rehearse it a little, make it look realistic like in Fight Club," Potbelly said.

"What's Fight Club?" Crazy Bob asked.

"I don't know; the first rule of Fight Club is that we are not supposed to talk about Fight Club," Potbelly said.

18

Chapter 5

The great riot of 2015 never occurred, because during their rehearsal of it, Potbelly sprained his thumb. He didn't have his thumb tucked in tight when he made his fist so when he swung, Crazy Bob moved out of the way and Potbelly's fist hit the table. The second rule of Fight Club, they decided, was to make a proper fist.

"What's on the agenda today?" Crazy Bob said.

"I hope we're not making friendship bracelets again," Drake said.

"I know, mine never turn out right," Potbelly said.

"Why can't we make an acquaintance bracelet for once?" Crazy Bob said.

"I don't think those sell as well," Drake said.

"They sell our friendship bracelets?" Crazy Bob was stunned.

"Of course, why do you think we make them?" Drake said.

"To hand them out to friends," Crazy Bob said.

"There's no money to be made in making friendship bracelets and then turning around and giving them to friends for free," Drake said.

"I can't make one; my thumb is sprained," Potbelly said.

"I think I sprained my thumb too," Crazy Bob said.

"How did you sprain your thumb?" Potbelly asked. "You didn't even take a swing."

"I took a swing at a stink bug that was in my room yesterday," Crazy Bob said.

"Did you hit it?" Potbelly asked.

"I did and it farted on my hand. Here, smell."

Crazy Bob stuck his hand under Potbelly's nose.

"Ugh, that's rancid. It smells like you've been wiping yourself with that hand," Potbelly said.

"Well, I have; but that's not really the point, though, is it?" Crazy Bob said.

"What is the point?" Drake asked.

"The point is, this place is a sweat shop. We have to make things for them to sell, and we don't even get paid for our work," Crazy Bob said.

"I have noticed that you sweat a lot," Drake said.

Crazy Bob wiped his forehead on the sleeve of his flannel shirt.

"I don't even like our work," Potbelly said.

"How much do they sell our bracelets for?" Crazy Bob asked.

"Most of ours sell for $10, but yours usually sell for around $40," Drake said.

"Why do mine sell for so much more?" Crazy Bob asked.

Drake and Potbelly just looked at one another. They didn't want to offend their friend.

"You're kind of famous," Drake said.

"How am I famous?" Crazy Bob asked.

"Well, people seem to want to buy a bracelet from the Butcher of Browning Street," Drake said.

"Who the hell is that?" Crazy Bob asked.

"That is what the media called you after you killed your wife, and I guess the name has earned notoriety over the years," Drake said.

"But I didn't kill my wife," Crazy Bob said.

"We know that; it's just that other people seem to think it is true," Potbelly said.

Crazy Bob hung his head. He didn't want to be known as the Butcher of Browning Street or of any street. He wanted to be famous for something good.

Nurse Lovington squeaked through the door carrying a basket full of materials.

"We're going to make paint and/or draw on t-shirts today," she said.

Potbelly held up a bandaged thumb.

"I won't be able to draw."

Crazy Bob reached into his pocket to pull out some tissues which he wrapped around his thumb and held it up.

"I sprained my thumb too."

"Okay, Potbelly and Crazy Bob, you both can skip today's craft," Nurse Lovington said.

"If zey don't haf to make one, den vy should I?" Fritz van Schnitzelhoff asked.

"No one wants your Nazi t-shirts anyway," Drake said.

"I don't want to draw on t-shirts either; I want a soda," Abram yelled.

"I don't like to do this work. It makes me feel like a big jerk," Sam said.

"If we don't make t-shirts, the Canadians will win the Cold War," Lester said.

That got everyone going. Even Crazy Bob and Potbelly sat down to make a design. No one wanted the Canadians to win the Cold War. No one knew what the Cold War was or where Canada was on the map, for that matter; but it was all about patriotism and who made the better t-shirts.

Crazy Bob kept getting the tissue on his thumb stuck to the paint brush so he took off his bandage.

They each worked vigorously to make a t-shirt. Fritz got a little more creative this time; there were only so many swastikas one could make. He made an eagle, and its talons were clutching an iron cross. That's what he said it was, but to everyone else it looked like a bat on a broom; and since it was so close to Halloween, it would probably sell very well.

Potbelly drew the biggest pig anyone had ever seen with a cartoon bubble around his mouth with the words "It's a lifestyle choice."

Sam painted a giant eye with the caption "The eye sees you. The eye sees true." Whether he meant the eye of God, Sauron or the government was a mystery. It looked a little like the eye of Big Brother, only less threatening because it was kind of droopy. It was Big Brother's other, lazier eye.

Lester drew a flag with a maple leaf and wrote, "Blame Canada."

Joseph didn't draw or paint anything on his; he left it blank. It was a bold statement. It said we are nothing; I am nothing; life is just a random series of events and then we die; it is a void. It either meant that, or he didn't feel like doing any work.

Crazy Bob was sweating; he couldn't think of anything. It was hard to work under these conditions. The pressure to always produce, the deadlines; it was endless.

"This is like trying to work in Room 101," he murmured.

"What's in room 101?" Potbelly asked.

"It's that room in *The Shining* where the old chick with the saggy boobs is in the bathtub," Drake said.

"No, it's the room in George Orwell's novel *1984* where the worst things in the world happen. It was where the thought police tortured you. That is the worst room in the world," Crazy Bob said.

"Tortured you with what?" Potbelly asked.

"With whatever you are most afraid of," Crazy Bob said.

"I'm most afraid of going into a room where there is an old chick with saggy boobs in the bathtub," Drake said.

"Me too—and spiders," Potbelly said.

"This is my worst fear: working endlessly for a corporation that doesn't pay or reward you. A corporation that only has a bottom line," Crazy Bob said.

He splashed paint on the shirt and held it up.

"There, it's the new Picasso. Art is subjective, after all. Here, Nurse Lovington, this should fetch you a million dollars."

Nurse Lovington patted Crazy Bob on the back; she could tell he was in an agitated state. Crazy Bob began to sob.

"I am not a butcher; I don't even like to handle raw meat."

"I think that's enough activity for one day. Why don't you go to your room and rest?" Nurse Lovington said.

"I won't get any rest there; it's full of stink bugs," Crazy Bob said.

"You can rest in my room; my room is stink bug free," Potbelly said.

Nurse Lovington escorted Crazy Bob out of the dayroom.

"I'm worried about Crazy Bob; he seems crazier than usual," Potbelly said.

"Maybe he needs more drugs," Drake said.

"He is not taking any," Potbelly said.

"That's what I mean," Drake said.

"I need more drugs too," Potbelly said.

"We all need more drugs," Drake said.

"We need to plan an intervention for Crazy Bob," Potbelly said.

"What kind of intervention?" Drake asked.

"The kind of intervention that gets the person to take more drugs instead of less," Potbelly said.

"I don't think that's an intervention; I think that's called a party," Drake said.

"We need to plan the opposite of an intervention; we need a circumvention," Potbelly said.

"I don't want to cut Crazy Bob's penis," Drake said.

"We won't cut his penis; we will force drugs on him," Potbelly said.

"Okay, how?" Drake asked.

"By threatening to cut off his penis," Potbelly said.

Chapter 6

Crazy Bob woke up with a start. He had been dreaming he was a pirate. In the dream he was captain of the ship the *S.S. Nut House*. He had a peg leg, a pirate hat, a parrot on his shoulder and for some reason he was wearing an eye patch on both eyes.

That may have been why he woke up; he was steering the boat straight into the side of a cliff.

When he woke up, he didn't know where he was at first; and then he remembered he was in Potbelly's room.

He got up and went into his room. As soon as he opened the door, a pungent stench hit him square in the nose.

"God damn stink bugs," he said.

An imaginary one flew around his head, and he tried to swat it.

Drake and Potbelly burst into the room. They were both wearing ski masks. Potbelly was holding a pair of pliers, and Drake had an armful of pill bottles.

Potbelly pushed Crazy Bob on the bed and held down his arms.

"Take these pills or we cut off your penis," Drake said.

He said it in a deep voice, so Crazy Bob wouldn't recognize it. He sounded like Batman.

"What is this? Who are you? Why do you want me to take drugs, and why do you want to cut off my penis?" Crazy Bob said.

Potbelly had Crazy Bob's shoulders held down, and he was kicking and flailing.

"We are circumnavigators, and this is a circumvention," Drake said, using the Batman voice.

"You want me to take all of those pills?" Crazy Bob asked.

"Yes," Batman said.

"I'm boycotting all pills," Crazy Bob said.

"If you don't take them, my associate is going to cut your penis off with those pliers," Batman said.

"What are you going to do with my penis?" Crazy Bob asked.

"Nothing if you take the drugs now and going forward in the required dosages. If not, we cut your penis off and sell it on eBay," Batman said.

"How much money can you get for a penis on eBay?" Crazy Bob said.

"Well, like most things it depends on what condition it is in," Batman said.

"Mine has barely been used in the last thirty-five years," Crazy Bob said.

"There's that factor, and if it's been taken out of the box, etc.," Batman said.

"I take it out of my boxers every time I go to pee," Crazy Bob said.

"That will affect the price a little then," Batman said.

Potbelly nudged him because he was getting off-topic.

"Right, now I'm going to leave all these medications here and I suggest you take them. Don't try and throw them away or hide them because we will know if you've taken them or not," Batman said.

"How will you know?" Crazy Bob asked.

"The stink bugs will inform us; we have planted stink bug spies in your room," Batman said.

"I knew it! I knew these stink bugs were sent to spy on me. Are they from Canada? Are they sleeper agents?" Crazy Bob asked.

Drake had no idea what he was talking about.

"They sleep sometimes, mostly they just take siestas; but they are highly trained agents," Drake said.

He forgot to do the Batman voice that time.

"What's wrong with your voice?" Crazy Bob asked.

"Nothing, I accidentally swallowed a stink bug," Batman said.

Potbelly let Crazy Bob up; and as soon as he did, Crazy Bob punched him in the jaw.

Potbelly yelped and held his jaw but didn't say anything. He didn't think he could do the Batman voice so he remained silent.

"Remember, we will be watching you," Batman said.

Drake and Potbelly left the room.

Crazy Bob picked up some of the bottles.

Clozapine, Lexapro, Abilify—I don't even take half of these medications, he thought.

Singulair? Isn't that for asthma? He wondered.

He looked at the other bottles labeled Cialis, Viagra and Levitra which were all for erectile dysfunction.

He didn't want the stink bugs informing the circumnavigators that he didn't take the medications, so he got some water and took each one according to the instructions. He laid back down waiting for the medication to kick in. Half an hour later, he felt a confluence of emotions and physical effects. His mouth was dry; he felt excited and irritated; he felt shooting pains in his hip; he felt like his bowels were about to evacuate and above all he felt highly aroused as indicated by his very erect penis.

Crazy Bob grabbed a book and held it over his penis to try and hide the erection and ran down the hall to the bathroom.

When he got to the bathroom, there was a line. Lester was in the back of the line hunched over and clutching his stomach.

"What's going on? Why is there such a line to the bathroom?" Crazy Bob asked him.

"Isabel made her special chili for lunch," Lester said.

Abram, who was standing in front of the line, pounded on the door.

"Come on, Joseph; you've been in there ten minutes already."

Joseph didn't respond, so Abram opened the door.

"Come on out of there; other people need to use the facilities," Abram said as he yanked an imaginary arm up.

Abram closed the door and locked it, just in case anyone decided to barge in on him and yank him out.

"This is going to take forever; I can't wait any longer," Crazy Bob said.

He ran back down the hall and opened the broom closet. He pulled his pants down, which was hard to do because his penis was still at attention, and sat down on a wash bucket.

He was in there for a full twenty minutes before finally emerging from the closet. He put the book over his penis and ran back to his room. On the way back, he bumped into Dr. Boyd.

"Oh, there you are. Where have you been? We had an appointment half an hour ago," Dr. Boyd said.

Crazy Bob was trying his best to hide his erection with the book. Luckily he grabbed *War and Peace*; it would have been a lot harder to cover if he had grabbed a novella.

"I've been in the bathroom all this time; I'm not feeling well," Crazy Bob said.

"Ah, I suspect you are not the only one. Isabella made her infamous chili. I'm glad I brought a salad. Not to worry, we can reschedule," Dr. Boyd said.

"Thank you, yes, we can reschedule for later in the week," Crazy Bob said.

"What are you reading?" Dr. Boyd said.

"It's *War and Peace*," Crazy Bob said without raising the book.

"That's not a first edition, is it? It can't be. May I see it?" Dr. Boyd asked.

Dr. Boyd started to grab the book and tugged at it.

Crazy Bob tugged back.

"It's not a first edition; it's just an old copy," Crazy Bob said.

Dr. Boyd could see that Crazy Bob was in some distress and wanted to get back to his room.

"Okay, Robert, I'll check on you later when you're feeling better," Dr. Boyd said.

Crazy Bob rushed to his room and closed the door. He wished the doors had locks on them because he wanted some privacy. He lay down again and tried to fall asleep, but his penis was throbbing. He hadn't seen it this lively in a long time, so he decided there was only one thing to do.

The best thing to do was to draw a face on it and maybe even make a hat. He got a sharpie, some construction paper and a tube of glitter out of his desk drawer and began to work.

Chapter 7

Crazy Bob walked into the dayroom and saw Drake and Potbelly sitting down at their table. Crazy Bob had finally lost his erection; it might have been facilitated by the hot glue gun.

He wasn't taking any of the erectile dysfunction drugs anymore; he didn't care if the stink bugs informed the circumnavigators about it. It was probably an oversight anyway since there was obviously nothing wrong with his penis; it was in good working order.

Fritz van Schnitzelhoff was standing behind a podium speaking German, gesturing like a mad man with his hands and slapping the podium.

He wanted to look more like Adolf Hitler, but he had blonde hair and couldn't grow a mustache, only peach fuzz, so he had to settle for imitating him. He was giving his famous Nuremburg speech, only no one could understand what he was saying; and nobody was paying attention anyway.

Crazy Bob noticed Potbelly's swollen jaw right away.

"What happened to you?" he asked.

Potbelly said the first thing that came to his mind because he had not thought of a plausible cover story yet.

"I was in the middle of a jealous lovers' quarrel," Potbelly said.

Drake nudged him.

"I mean I got hit with a door knob," Potbelly said.

"Which is it, a door knob or a jealous lovers' quarrel?" Crazy Bob asked.

"Neither. I mean both," Potbelly said.

Drake changed the subject; he could see that Potbelly was about to fold under questioning.

"How are you feeling? You look a lot better since we saw you last," Drake said.

"It's the damndest thing; two circumnavigators barged in my room, demanding that I take medication or they would cut off my penis with a pair of pliers," Crazy Bob said.

"What's a circumnavigator?" Drake asked.

"Someone who gives circumcisions obviously," Crazy Bob said.

"Obviously," Potbelly repeated.

"One of them was Batman, though; I could tell by his voice," Crazy Bob said.

"Batman threatened to cut off your penis?" Potbelly asked.

27

"I know; I was as surprised as you. I thought he was on the side of the law, but clearly that doesn't pay very well," Crazy Bob said.

"Did you take the medications?" Drake asked.

"Yes, I did, even the ones for erectile dysfunction," Crazy Bob said.

"You idiot! Why did you give him medication for erectile dysfunction?" Drake asked Potbelly.

"What did you say?" Crazy Bob asked.

"He said, 'It's a good thing you weren't hurt,'" Potbelly said.

"I didn't go down without a fight, though; I punched one of them in the jaw," Crazy Bob said.

He looked at the bruise on Potbelly's jaw.

"I hit him square in the jaw, right in the same spot that Potbelly got hit by the jealous lovers' doorknob. It must be a coincidence," Crazy Bob said.

"What's a coincidence?" Potbelly asked.

"That you got hit in the same place in the same day as the circumnavigator," Crazy Bob said.

"No, I meant, 'What does *coincidence* mean?'" Potbelly asked.

"I have no idea," Crazy Bob said.

"I didn't hit Batman, though; I hit the other one, the one who didn't talk," Crazy Bob said.

"I don't blame you; Batman probably knows karate," Potbelly said.

"I'd like to be a circumnavigator for a living; it would be much better than this place," Crazy Bob said.

"You'd rather go around masked and threatening people to take medication?" Drake asked.

"Yeah, think of all the traveling you could do and the people you'd meet," Crazy Bob said.

"I suppose you would meet a lot of people, albeit under hostile circumstances," Drake said.

"How much do you think that pays?" Potbelly asked.

"I don't know, but it's bound to be more than this place does," Crazy Bob said.

"We don't get paid anything," Drake said.

"That's what I mean," Crazy Bob said.

"Uhm, so if you're not going to take them, can I have some of those medications for erectile dysfunction?" Potbelly asked.

"Is your erectile dysfunctioning on you?" Crazy Bob asked.

"Yes, most days," Potbelly said.

Crazy Bob looked up at Fritz, who was still screaming in German and frothing at the mouth. He had a hand on each side of the podium, and he was gripping it so hard it looked like he was trying to snap it in two.

"What's Fritz talking about?" Crazy Bob asked.

"I have no idea; I don't think he is speaking American," Potbelly said.

Crazy Bob started to boo really loudly, and everyone else began joining in.

Fritz realized they were booing him and began slamming his fists down.

"Ztop, I am trying to make an important zpeech!" Fritz yelled.

The booing got so loud that Fritz could no longer continue.

"I don't haf to putz up vith dis."

Fritz went over to the tape recorder and shut it off. He then pulled out a tape labeled, "Adolf Hitler—Nuremburg." He had only been lip-syncing Hitler's famous Nuremburg speech.

Chapter 8

Drake was crazy, but he wasn't sure why he was crazy. The doctors weren't sure why he was crazy either. He had been in the looney bin for twenty-five years and never once been diagnosed. No one knew why Drake was there, not even Drake. Dr. Olive found it troubling that he had not been diagnosed yet after all these years, so he officially wrote up his diagnosis as "crazy with acute eccentricity." Both Drake and the doctors were satisfied with this diagnosis.

"How have you been feeling?" Dr. Olive asked.

"I feel much better now that I know what's wrong with me. Which should we work on treating first: my craziness or my eccentricity?" Drake asked.

"I think your eccentricity would be the easiest. What are some of your hobbies?" Dr. Olive asked.

"I like to draw faces on eggs," Drake said.

"What kind of faces?" Dr. Olive asked.

"Any kind: I draw happy, sad, surprised, you name it," Drake said.

"I see; this is very good. Now we are getting to the root of your eccentricity. I would like for you to stop drawing faces on eggs for a while and see how you feel," Dr. Olive said.

"I like drawing faces on eggs, though," Drake said.

"Yes, but how do you expect to cure your eccentricity if you go around drawing faces on eggs?" Dr. Olive asked.

"What is wrong with being eccentric anyway? Weren't some of the greatest inventors eccentric?" Drake asked.

"I can't think of any," Dr. Olive said.

Dr. Olive looked at Drake over his horn-rimmed glasses; like his name, he had an olive complexion. His family was Cherokee Indian on his father's side. He had rich brown eyes, and like Dr. Boyd, he too was a bachelor; but unlike Dr. Boyd, he had lived away from home for a long time. He had had a string of unsuccessful relationships with women. Dr. Olive had a competitive side as well as a penchant for perfection, which caused him to be wound a little tightly. He never let his hair down, and the women found it boring.

"Well, what else should I do?" Drake asked.

"I think you should draw faces on paper instead," Dr. Olive said.

"I don't think I would like that as much," Drake said.

"Give it a try and see. The important thing is that you stop drawing the faces on eggs," Dr. Olive said.

"Are you sure that drawing faces on eggs is eccentric?" Drake asked.

"I'm quite sure; it's the most eccentric thing I've ever heard," Dr. Olive said.

"I don't know; I really like drawing faces on eggs, though. I'd hate to give it up. Are you sure there isn't some eccentric loop hole?" Drake asked.

"I tell you what; I'll consult with Dr. Boyd and get a second opinion. Would that make you feel better?" Dr. Olive asked.

"Yes, that would make me feel much better about giving up my hobby if I knew Dr. Boyd was in agreement," Drake said.

Dr. Olive hated Dr. Boyd and had no intention of asking him anything; he just said it to satisfy Drake.

"Where are you getting the eggs, by the way?" Dr. Olive asked.

"Isabella, the cook, gives them to me. I told her that I like to draw faces on them; and you know what? She now likes to draw faces on them too," Drake said.

"Interesting, perhaps she suffers from eccentricity too. Where do you put the eggs that you've drawn faces on?" Dr. Olive asked.

"I give them back to Isabella; I don't keep them. She uses them to make breakfast," Drake said.

"So you draw faces on the eggs, but you don't even save the eggs?" Dr. Olive asked.

"That's right. I guess I should tell Isabella to stop drawing faces on eggs too," Drake said.

"Isabella is not a patient and is not subject to the same rules. Besides, I think we should forget the whole thing. I think it is fine for you to draw faces on the eggs as long as you're not keeping them out for show, like a collection," Dr. Olive said.

"Why is it fine for me to draw the faces on eggs now?" Drake asked.

"Because I thought you were drawing the faces on the eggs and keeping them in your room on display. That would constitute as an eccentric hobby. You're drawing faces on eggs, only to turn around and give them back to Isabella to cook. That's not eccentric; that's crazy, and we are trying to cure you of eccentricity first," Dr. Olive said.

"Are you still going to consult with Dr. Boyd?" Drake asked.

"There's no need now because I don't believe that it is eccentric

31

behavior; I believe it is crazy behavior," Dr. Olive said.

"So what do we do now?" Drake asked.

"I guess we go back to the drawing board," Dr. Olive said.

"We go back to drawing faces on eggs," Drake said.

"Quite right," Dr. Olive said.

"I have some other hobbies; I like helping Crazy Bob look for stink bugs in his room," Drake said.

"What do you do with the stink bugs after you catch them?" Dr. Olive asked.

"I never find any," Drake said.

"So you look for stink bugs that aren't there?" Dr. Olive said.

"They are there; Crazy Bob says so. I just don't ever find any when I go to look for them; they are crafty bugs," Drake said.

"It sounds like it is a figment of Crazy Bob's imagination," Dr. Olive said.

"I don't think so; Crazy Bob doesn't even like figs," Drake said.

"No, I mean they don't really exist; they are just more of Crazy Bob's delusions," Dr. Olive said.

"Well, even though we don't find any, I still find it fun to look for them," Drake said.

"This really isn't eccentricity. It's madness, and it's not even your madness; it's Crazy Bob's," Dr. Olive said.

"I do other eccentric stuff," Drake said.

Dr. Olive looked at the owl clock on his desk. He was getting a little impatient. He loved birds, owls in particular. He was an avid bird watcher and liked to collect owl figurines. You might even say that he himself was eccentric; and it has been said many times by every girl he had ever gone out with.

"I think that's all the time we have for today, so you'll have to hold that thought for next time," Dr. Olive said.

Drake stayed seated in his chair, motionless. He just stared at Dr. Olive, and he looked as if he were concentrating on something really hard.

"I'm afraid we are out of time," Dr. Olive said.

"I know; I'm just holding my thoughts," Drake said.

"Okay, that's good. You can leave, though; it's okay to take your thoughts with you and bring them next time we meet," Dr. Olive said.

Drake rose from his chair. He brushed his curly red hair out of his eyes.

"Good idea. I think I could sit here and hold my thoughts until next time, but not my pee."

Chapter 9

"What are you writing down?" Drake asked.

"I'm writing down every conversation that I have," Crazy Bob said.

"Why would you want to do that?" Potbelly asked.

"I want to remember the conversations," Crazy Bob said.

"All of them?" Drake asked.

"Yes, they are important," Crazy Bob said.

"What's so important about your conversations that you need to remember?" Drake asked.

"I'm writing them down because Dr. Boyd writes all of our conversations down, and I think it's important to remember these things," Crazy Bob said.

"Dr. Olive doesn't write any of our conversations down," Drake said.

"Come to think of it; I don't think Dr. Olive writes mine down either," Potbelly said.

"Well, that's Dr. Olive. I'm talking about Dr. Boyd. I missed out on reading conversations of my first twenty-five years here so I'd like to start recording them for myself," Crazy Bob said.

"Are you writing every single word down that someone says to you?" Potbelly asked.

"Yes, that way I shall never forget it," Crazy Bob said.

"Even if someone asks you something mundane, like where the bathroom is, you're going to write that down?" Drake asked.

"That's right; no information is too mundane as far as I'm concerned. You never know when you might need it for later," Crazy Bob said.

"What if you're talking to a stranger that you'll probably never see again? Are you going to write that down too?" Potbelly asked.

"Yes, everything," Crazy Bob said.

"What do you have in there so far?" Potbelly asked.

"I wrote down what we have been talking about the last five minutes. This is my first entry into the notebook," Crazy Bob said.

"So you wrote down in your notebook the fact that you are going to be writing stuff down in your notebook?" Drake asked.

"That's right," Crazy Bob said.

Nurse Lovington approached their table. Her white uniform was stained around the collar; it was in desperate need of bleaching. Her white shoes squeaked loudly every time she took a step. Nurse Lovington had shoulder-length brown hair; she was in her early thirties. She had smooth, creamy skin and a clear complexion; but she was a little on the plump side. She was engaged to a stock broker, but he eloped with her best friend; that was six months and ten pounds ago. Since then, she had taken little pride in her appearance; she stopped wearing makeup, and she didn't care if her uniform were stained or her shoes squeaky. She decided it wasn't worth the effort.

"It's time to take your medicine," Nurse Lovington said.

"I'm boycotting all medicine," Crazy Bob said.

"You can't boycott your medicine; you are a paranoid schizophrenic who suffers from delusions of grandeur," Nurse Lovington said.

"I'm not paranoid," Crazy Bob said.

"All paranoid people say that," Nurse Lovington said.

"I don't have delusions of grandeur either," Crazy Bob said.

"Of course you do, you and your stink bugs," Nurse Lovington said.

"The correct term is fart bugs, and they are crawling everywhere in my room," Crazy Bob said.

"You need to take your medicine," Nurse Lovington said.

"No, I'm boycotting all medicine," Crazy Bob said.

"What about the circumnavigators?" Drake asked.

"Oh, right, I forgot about them. Okay, Nurse Lovington, you can give me the medication," Crazy Bob said.

"What are circumnavigators?" Nurse Lovington asked.

"They're like pirates, except instead of stealing gold, they steal your penis," Potbelly said.

"Don't be silly; who would want Crazy Bob's penis?" Nurse Lovington asked.

"I want my penis," Crazy Bob said.

Nurse Lovington handed Potbelly his pills and a cup of water.

Potbelly examined them in his hands. There was one yellow pill and two pink pills. He shoved them all in his mouth at the same time and took a chug of water.

"Here, take your pill too."

Nurse Lovington gave a pill to Drake.

"I don't take any pills," Drake said.

"You do now. Dr. Olive says you're crazy with acute

eccentricity. He says you need to take this pill," Nurse Lovington said.

"I don't want to take any medicine," Drake said.

"I didn't say it was medicine; I said it was a pill," Nurse Lovington said.

"If it's not medicine, what is it then?" Drake asked.

"It's a placebo; there's no medicine in it," Nurse Lovington said.

"Why do I have to take a pill if there is nothing in it?" Drake asked.

"You have craziness with acute eccentricity, so you have to take something; and since Dr. Olive has no idea what that something should be, he's giving you a placebo," Nurse Lovington said.

"But if it's a placebo, it's not going to help my craziness or my eccentricity," Drake protested.

"But it won't hurt it either. So take it."

Nurse Lovington thrust the pill on the table in front of him, along with the water.

Drake reluctantly put the placebo in his mouth and washed it down with the water.

"I am taking my pills, but I am not a paranoid schizomatic," Crazy Bob said.

"It's paranoid schizophrenic," Nurse Lovington said.

"Confounded woman, I'm not paranoid; those damn fart bugs are crawling all over my room and farting up the place," Crazy Bob said.

Nurse Lovington just shook her head and squeaked away in her squeaky shoes.

"Hey, you forgot to write down the conversation you had with Nurse Lovington," Potbelly said.

"Damn, does anyone recall how it went?" Crazy Bob asked.

"I believe she told you to take your medicine, and you said that you were boycotting all medicine; and then I reminded you of the circumnavigators," Drake said.

"Yeah and then she called you a paranoid socialist," Potbelly said.

"What is a paranoid socialist?" Crazy Bob asked.

"It means you have a mistrust of others and believe they are conspiring against you. However, those same people who are conspiring against you should be able to own things collectively for a common benefit," Drake said.

"That's quite right. I do have a natural distrust of others but see no reason why they can't enjoy all the same benefits that I enjoy," Crazy Bob said.

"I think I'm a paranoid socialist too," Drake said.

"Me too," Potbelly said.

"By god, we should all be paranoid socialists. The world would be a much better place," Crazy Bob said.

"You forgot to write that down," Drake pointed out.

"Damn, this is going to be harder than I thought," Crazy Bob said.

Chapter 10

"I would very much like you to change my diagnosis from crazy with acute eccentricity to paranoid socialist," Drake said.

"I don't think that is a real diagnosis," Dr. Olive said.

"Well, neither is crazy with acute eccentricity," Drake said.

"Why don't you just become a socialist? It would be easier than changing your diagnosis," Dr. Olive said.

"I already am a socialist," Drake said.

"Then you don't need to have your diagnosis changed, do you?" Dr. Olive asked.

"But I don't want to be just a socialist; I want to be paranoid as well," Drake said.

"You can be paranoid all you like. Lots of people are paranoid; I'm paranoid," Dr. Olive said.

"I want it to be my diagnosis, just like Crazy Bob's," Drake said.

"Robert isn't a paranoid socialist," Dr. Olive said.

"Yes, he is; Nurse Lovington said so," Drake said.

"Nurse Lovington is mistaken then. Robert is a paranoid schizophrenic," Dr. Olive said.

"What's a schizophrenic?" Drake asked.

"It's a disorder that makes it hard to tell the difference between what is real and not real," Dr. Olive said.

"Crazy Bob knows what's real and not real," Drake said.

"No, he doesn't. Why else would he see stink bugs that aren't really there?" Dr. Olive said.

"He doesn't see stink bugs; he sees fart bugs," Drake said.

"Either way, they aren't there," Dr. Olive said.

"How do you know they aren't there?" Drake asked.

"Because you haven't been able to find any, and Nurse Lovington has looked several times and not been able to find a single one," Dr. Olive said.

"Nurse Lovington can't find any books on pot-bellied pigs; she can't even find the new patient Godot," Drake said.

"What new patient Godot?" Dr. Olive asked.

"The new one that Crazy Bob is waiting for; he hasn't shown up yet," Drake said.

"I wasn't aware of any new patient, especially one named Godot," Dr. Olive said.

"It sounds like no one knows what's going on around here except

38

for Crazy Bob; and he's crazy," Drake said.

"I assure you that I have a good handle on what goes on around here," Dr. Olive said.

"I want to be a paranoid socialist," Drake said.

"You can be a paranoid socialist; no one is stopping you," Dr. Olive said.

"I want it to be my diagnosis, though," Drake said.

"It can't be your diagnosis," Dr. Olive said

"Why not?" Drake asked.

"Because socialism is unpatriotic, that's why," Dr. Olive said.

"Why is it unpatriotic?" Drake asked.

"Because there is a war going on," Dr. Olive said.

"What war?" Drake asked.

"I don't know; there's probably a war going on somewhere in the world, though," Dr. Olive said.

"So you won't change my diagnosis?" Drake asked.

"We will have to leave it as it is, or the best I can do is to change it to paranoid capitalist," Dr. Olive said.

"What does that mean?" Drake asked.

"It means you still have an unreasonable distrust of others; but you believe the investment, the means of production, distribution and exchange of wealth should be maintained by individuals and corporations," Dr. Olive said.

"But I believe my mistrust in capitalists isn't unreasonable," Drake said.

"If I change your diagnosis to paranoid capitalist, then that means you are cured of your eccentricity and have moved on to something better," Dr. Olive said.

"What about my craziness?" Drake asked.

"I'm afraid that is incurable; you are stuck with that," Dr. Olive said.

"What else can you offer me?" Drake asked.

"If you're a paranoid capitalist, you can invest in our corporation," Dr. Olive said.

"What corporation?" Drake asked.

"Why, the Looney Bin, of course," Dr. Olive said.

"The Looney Bin is a corporation?" Drake asked.

"Sure it is; why do you think we are called Looney Bin Inc.?" Dr. Olive asked.

"I didn't know we were called that," Drake said.

"It is written in big letters right outside our doors," Dr. Olive said.

"I haven't been outside our doors in twenty-five years," Drake said.

"Oh yes, well, twenty-five years ago, we would have been Looney Bin LLC. We became incorporated for tax purposes. We even have our own letterhead," Dr. Olive said.

Dr. Olive handed Drake a sheet of paper. Drake examined it.

Looney Bin Incorporated. Making crazy a mission since 1958.

"I can't make out the company logo," Drake said.

"It's a picture of a man in a strait jacket," Dr. Olive said.

"Will I still have to take a placebo?" Drake asked.

"No, you don't take them. You sell them, of course, like any good capitalist," Dr. Olive said.

"It's a deal then. I am now a crazy paranoid capitalist," Drake said, beaming.

"I will write it down and make it official," Dr. Olive said.

He wrote it on the company letterhead right underneath the company logo of the man in the strait jacket and then signed his name.

Chapter 11

Looney Bin Incorporated was a highly profitable chain of insane asylums. It first began as a small mom-and-pop insane asylum; but through ruthless exploitation of its workers and extremely low overhead, it rapidly grew into a conglomerate.

Their commercials had a catchy jingle:

Come on out and don't be lazy,
if you know you're really crazy.
Anxiety and OCD, we want you.
Bipolar, schizophrenia and depressives too.
So listen to those voices inside your heads,
because Looney Bin Inc. has got your meds.

The board was having their quarterly board meeting. Dr. Raven, who had been on the board for twenty years, was the chairman. The meeting was being held in their New York headquarters in a sleek, modern building on the top floor. All twelve board members were present and listening attentively to Dr. Raven.

"Since we started a division of Looney Bin Incorporated for women, our profits have quadrupled. I think we should expand to children as well," Dr. Raven said.

"I agree; children today are already on a lot of medication, so why not have let them stay in a mental institution while they're at it?" Dr. Sherman said.

"Parents might not go for that; today's parents like their kids drugged up but still want them at home so they can take them to their horseback riding lessons, soccer games and ballet recitals. I don't think they will go for extended stays," Dr. Johnson said.

"That's why I was thinking we could make them short stays like a summer camp; each week we could have a theme. One week we could have a crazy in Hawaii theme where the kids could have a luau and wear grass skirts. Another week we could have an outer space theme and so forth," Dr. Raven said.

"We could even do birthday parties," Dr. Johnson added.

"I think it's a good idea," Dr. Sherman said.

"Shall we put it to a vote? Dr. Yardley, if you please," Dr. Raven said.

"All those in favor of starting a new children's division?" Dr. Yardley asked.

41

It was unanimous but just for form's sake, he asked, "All those opposed?"

Dr. Yardley, who kept the minutes of the board meetings, jotted down the results.

"Great, I'll have a team work up some projections for next time. Our next order of business is one of our branches in Pennsylvania. It is consistently one of our most profitable. I've read some of the patients' files from Dr. Boyd, one of the doctors on staff; and I think it would be great to have the patients there in our next commercial," Dr. Raven said.

"We could have a camera crew out there as early as next week," Dr. Sherman said.

"How about we put it to a vote?" Dr. Raven said.

"All those in favor?" Dr. Yardley asked.

All the hands went up. Dr. Yardley didn't know why they ever bothered taking a vote; no one ever disagreed with Dr. Raven.

Dr. Jared Raven was the son of Dr. Lloyd Raven, the original founding member of Looney Bin Inc. He was number fifteen on Forbes' list of richest men in the world. He gave millions to his favorite charity each year, Crazy without Borders. It is a nonprofit organization that helps provide medication and services to mentally ill adults and children in poor countries.

It was a charity he founded, and he also sits on the board. Dr. Jared was always looking to expand the company's profits; he had taken the company to a whole new level. His father, had he still been living, would have been very proud.

He sipped on his tea and shoved a pineapple wedge in his mouth. The receptionist had the food catered from one of the finest restaurants in New York. They had their quarterly meetings in a different location every time. Next quarter it would be in Tokyo; and at the end of the year, it was going to be in Bermuda.

Yes indeed, it was nothing but the best for the board of Looney Bin Incorporated, who had not only been making crazy a mission since 1958 but making money as well.

No company was better at cutting costs and creating revenue. It was one of the only companies that didn't pay ninety percent of its workers. No other company could get away with that, and few have tried. Workers will work even when they are not making a living wage; but none will work for free, unless, of course, they are crazy. Fortunately, most all of their employees were. It was the era for unprecedented control by corporations, and Looney Bin Incorporated was riding the wave.

Chapter 12

"Do you think it might be a good idea to cut back on the soda?" Dr. Boyd asked.

"Cut back—what do you mean? I never get any soda, so how can I cut back?" Abram asked.

"I meant cut back on your need for soda," Dr. Boyd said.

"How do I do that?" Abram asked.

"Have you tried crack?" Dr. Boyd asked.

"The vending machines only have food and drink; they don't carry crack," Abram said.

"I'll call the vending machine company and see what we can do. Meanwhile, let's try to get at the root of your soda addiction psychologically," Dr. Boyd said.

"You said your mother and father didn't let you have sugary drinks as a kid?" Dr. Boyd asked.

"Yes, no sugary drinks, television, radio, electricity or anything remotely interesting. We were Amish," Abram said.

"You must have had a stern childhood with lots of rules," Dr. Boyd said.

"Yes, there were tons of rules and a lot of hard work. I worked six days a week from sunup to sundown," Abram said.

"What kind of work did you do?" Dr. Boyd asked.

"I did whatever needed doing. I worked in the garden, did carpentry, you name it," Abram said.

"So you developed a good work ethic?" Dr. Boyd asked.

"Yes, for all the good it does me here," Abram said.

"What do you mean?" Dr. Boyd asked.

"I mean sleeping in until 10 a.m., making friendship bracelets and t-shirts and listening to Crazy Bob's crackpot theories hardly takes any work ethic," Abram said.

"So you're afraid of leisure time; you're afraid you might have too much time for reflection and introspection?" Dr. Boyd asked.

"I'm just bored, Doc," Abram said.

Dr. Boyd flipped through Abram's chart.

"You were diagnosed by your last hospital as having dissociative boredom disorder," Dr. Boyd said.

"Yes, I was bored there too. Do you think my problem might be that I just need a challenge, more stimulation?" Abram asked.

"No, I think you need drugs," Dr. Boyd said.

"I thought you said that you wanted to get to the root of my problem psychologically," Abram said.

"Yes, but that would be time-consuming and boring; and it seems you're bored enough as it is," Dr. Boyd said.

"Yes, I'm very bored; I'm consumed with it," Abram said.

"I'm going to give you Risperdal," Dr. Boyd said.

"Isn't that an antipsychotic?" Abram asked.

"It is but prolonged boredom can lead to delusions of grandeur, so we want to head that off. Risperdal will work fine until the crack arrives," Dr. Boyd said. "Okay, Abram, it looks like we are out of time."

"But we still have twenty minutes," Abram said.

"I know, but I wouldn't want you to get bored; it might start triggering delusions," Dr. Boyd said.

When Abram left Dr. Boyd's office, he felt better; but he still really wanted a soda. His body was craving some caffeine.

He went into the break room and paused in front of the soda machine. He stood in front of it staring at it; a pool of sweat began to form around his brow, and his hand twitched like a gunslinger in the old west who was about to have a duel.

Abram reached into his pocket and pulled out some change. He put the quarter in and waited. The machine did not spit the quarter back out, so he tried the next quarter. It accepted that quarter as well, so then he tried the dime; but the machine wouldn't take it. He tried to insert the dime again, but the machine refused it again.

Abram examined the dime; it was made right here in the good ole USA and it didn't have any smudges on it.

What is the problem then? He wondered.

He reached into his pocket and pulled out two nickels. Abram tried two nickels instead, but the machine wasn't fooled; it spat them back out so hard they landed in the floor.

He couldn't take it; it was just too much for him, so he lay down on the floor and started writhing as if he were in agony and yelling at the top of his lungs.

"It isn't fair!"

The yelling soon caught the attention of others. Crazy Bob grabbed his notebook and pen and followed the crowd that was headed into the break room. He walked behind Lester who was hunched over and walking on his tippy toes, like he was taking part in one of his imaginary CIA stealth operations. Nurse Lovington

45

squeaked on over to see what all the commotion was about.

"Here comes Sneaky and Squeaky," Drake said.

"I didn't put any Canadian money in the machine this time, and it still refuses to take my money," Abram shouted.

No one was sure why the soda machine was even there because Abram was the only person who ever wanted a soda, and he never got a single one. Even so, a man with the vending machine company came by periodically to collect the money, but he never had to refill the machine. Dr. Boyd and Dr. Olive arrived carrying a hypodermic needle in each hand. They had enough sedative in their syringes to knock out a beached whale, let alone a beached Abram, who was five feet tall with a hundred-pound frame.

Abram waved away the doctors, who were ready to pounce on him if he didn't calm down.

Abram stood up to demonstrate. He put all his change in, and the machine spat it back out. He tried again, and still the machine burped it up like it had eaten enough and it was full.

Crazy Bob came over to examine one of the nickels.

"It is an American nickel alright. It looks like it has a smudge on it, though," Crazy Bob said.

"No, it doesn't. This machine just hates me," Abram said.

Crazy Bob held his notebook against the machine and began to write.

"Machines don't like or dislike people, Abram; they don't have feelings," Dr. Boyd said.

"This one does; it hates me. It's never given me a soda," Abram said.

"Why should it give you a soda? It isn't a paranoid socialist; it's a paranoid capitalist like me," Drake said.

"Drake has a good point there, Abram. If the machine were a paranoid socialist like me, it would be happy to give you a soda," Crazy Bob said.

"But I'm paying money for a commodity; isn't that the essence of capitalism?" Abram asked.

"Yes, but are you paying enough? The demand of soda determines the market price," Drake said.

"What demand? I'm the only one who wants to buy one. I'm putting in sixty cents, the amount it requires," Abram said.

He put the nickel in again and watched it fall back out. Then he started to scream and bang his head on the machine. "I want my soda; I want my soda."

Dr. Boyd and Dr. Olive wasted no time in giving him a shot. The two doctors carried him away, and Nurse Lovington squeaked after them.

"Poor Abram, all he wants in life is a soda; and the machine refuses to give him one," Potbelly said.

"Nothing in life is given to you; you have to earn it," Drake said.

"I don't think that's how it works with soda machines," Crazy Bob said.

"Of course it is; soda machines are no exception," Drake said.

"Hey, are you still waiting for that patient Godot?" Lester asked.

"Who wants to know?" Crazy Bob asked.

"I want to know; that's why I asked," Lester said.

"Yes, we are still waiting for him," Crazy Bob said.

"Well, I've found out some news about him. Do you want to hear it?" Lester asked.

Lester had a borderline personality disorder, and in addition to that, he was a Sagittarius; and in addition to that addition, he was a big fat liar.

Crazy Bob only smiled.

"The reason he hasn't been admitted yet is because they think he might have leprosy," Lester said.

"People still get leprosy?" Potbelly asked.

"Of course they do. You can get them from armadillos," Lester said.

"Was he in contact with an armadillo?" Drake asked.

"He had an armadillo as a pet," Lester said.

"He should have gotten a pot-bellied pig. Armadillos are known to carry all kinds of diseases," Potbelly said.

"I heard that he lost his index finger on his right hand, and Nurse Lovington had to glue it back on," Lester said.

"How does he pick his nose?" Potbelly asked.

"I guess he can't," Lester said.

"How did the armadillo get leprosy? I thought only leopards carried leprosy," Crazy Bob said.

"It was probably a spotted armadillo," Potbelly said.

"You said they think he might have leprosy. What else could he possibly have that would make a finger fall off?" Crazy Bob asked.

"My grandmother had gum disease, and all her teeth fell out," Drake said.

"Maybe Godot has gum disease," Potbelly said.

"Is gum disease contagious?" Crazy Bob asked.

"It's highly contagious; that's why they have to quarantine him, so they can figure out if he has it or not," Lester said.

"I don't want to wait for Godot anymore. He might be admitted and give us all gum disease," Potbelly said.

"I don't mind waiting for him. I'm getting out of here the day that comes after the day after tomorrow, so he won't have time to give it to me," Crazy Bob said.

"I suggest the rest of you stop waiting for him then," Lester said.

"Well, if we aren't going to wait for him anymore, who can we wait for?" Drake asked.

"We could always wait for Virgil to get out of solitary confinement," Potbelly said.

"I heard he has penile dysfunction," Lester said.

Everyone grabbed their crotches to safeguard them, just in case penile dysfunction had anything to do with your penis falling off.

"I don't think that's contagious," Crazy Bob said.

"The rare kind he has is highly contagious. It's called rare highly-contagious penile dysfunction," Lester said.

"So many diseases around here; it almost makes you wish you weren't a crazy paranoid capitalist," Drake said.

"How are things in the Canadian Cold War?" Potbelly asked.

"It's still a tie, but I have a plan to win the war with those hockey-loving bastards once and for all," Lester said.

"I like hockey," Drake said.

"What's the plan?" Crazy Bob asked.

"It's top secret. I could tell you, but then I'd have to kill you and put you in jail. In that order," Lester said.

"Can you give as a hint then?" Crazy Bob asked.

"It involves the Queen of England, but that's all I'm going to say," Lester said.

"What's the Queen of England got to do with Canada?" Potbelly asked.

"I loved her song, 'Fat Bottom Girls,'" Crazy Bob said.

"If I tell you, then the terrorists win. Do you want the terrorists to win?" Lester asked.

Crazy Bob, Potbelly and Drake shook their heads; they definitely did not want the terrorists to win.

Chapter 13

It was circle time. It was a time when Nurse Lovington went around to each person in the group and let them share something.

Mostly it was a time for Potbelly to talk about pot-bellied pigs. It was the worst of times; it was the worst of times.

"Pot-bellied pigs are the same species as ordinary farm yard pigs and wild boars, so they are capable of interbreeding," Potbelly said.

"Don't Jew ever talk aboutz anysing elze? I am zick of hearing about potz-bellied pigz. Who carez aboutz dem?" Fritz van Schnitzelhoff asked.

"Heil Hitler," Crazy Bob stood up and saluted.

"How many timez do I haf to tell you moronz dat I'm not German. My family iz frum de Netherlandz. I haf obzezzive compulzive dizorder and chronic hemorrhoidz, but I am notz a Nazi," Fritz said.

"You're a chronic Teutonic," Crazy Bob said.

"Give Richard a chance to speak; he has another minute left," Nurse Lovington said.

"Who's Richard?" Crazy Bob asked.

"I'm Richard," Potbelly said.

"Oh, right," Crazy Bob said.

Crazy Bob had his notebook and pencil with him, and he was keeping track of the conversations. He was having trouble writing everything down fast enough as it was being spoken. He was scribbling frantically. He paused for a second to review his writing.

PB said, "Pigs are not ordinary pigs; they intermarry."

Fritz said, "Don't Jews ever talk about anything, something, something...Nazi."

There was also something about hemorrhoids and then laughing.

Crazy Bob had no idea what it all meant.

"As I was saying, pot-bellied pigs can breed with regular pigs and wild boars. I recommend spaying or neutering them if you don't wish to breed them," Potbelly said.

"Okay, very good. Joseph, would you like to speak?" Nurse Lovington asked.

Joseph didn't want to speak; he never wanted to speak. In fact, Joseph had never spoken a word because Joseph was invisible; but everyone knew he was there nonetheless.

"Abram, would you like to say something?" Nurse Lovington asked.

"Yes, I would like to get a new soda machine in the break room. The one we have now is a fascist machine and won't give me any soda," Abram said.

Fritz's ears perked up.

"It really is a fascist?" Fritz asked.

"Clearly," Abram said.

"I don't know, Abram; that's quite an expense. I'll have to ask Dr. Boyd and Dr. Olive about it and see if it's in our budget. Is there anything else you'd like to say?" Nurse Lovington asked.

"No, that's it," Abram said.

"Alright, do you have anything to say Robert?" Nurse Lovington asked.

"Who's Robert?" Crazy Bob asked.

"You're Robert," Nurse Lovington said.

"Oh, right. I'd like to talk about fart bugs. They are sneaky little devils, and I can't seem to catch one. I'm offering a small monetary award if someone can catch one, so I can present it to the doubting Thomas, Dr. Boyd," Crazy Bob said.

"What's monetary mean?" Potbelly asked.

"It's like dysentery, only you just get it once instead of having it forever," Drake said.

"That sounds like a bargain; I'd rather have it once and get it over with than have it forever," Potbelly said.

"How about you Sam, would you like to speak today?" Nurse Lovington asked.

"Who's Sam?" Crazy Bob asked.

"Sam is Sam," Drake said.

"Oh, right," Crazy Bob said.

Sam was obsessed with talking in rhymes, after he read the Dr. Seuss book *Green Eggs and Ham* and discovered he was the central character.

"Yes, I would like to talk. I would like to talk about chalk. Chalk can be all colors, even red, white and blue. Chalk can be small or large; chalk can even be old or new," Sam said.

Everyone stood up and clapped. It was momentous; it was absolute poetry. No one knew that chalk had such dimensions; no one had ever thought about chalk until now.

Sam felt encouraged and continued with a smile.

"I like chalk; I like it a lot, even though some of you may not," Sam said.

Everyone stood up to protest. They assured him that there was no one here who did not like chalk. They all liked chalk very much.

"Chalk can write and scribble and draw. To not have chalk should be against the law," Sam said.

Everyone agreed; it should be against the law.

"A world without chalk would be very sad; but a world with chalk makes me very glad," Sam said.

They all stood up to cheer once more. Sam stood up at the thunderous applause and took a bow. Nurse Lovington waited 'til the applause died down.

"Alright, Fritz, would you like to speak now?" Nurse Lovington asked.

"Oh zure, now Jew wantz me to zpeak. How am I zuppozed to follow dat? I am not a poet; I can't zpeak eloquent wordz," Fritz said.

"Okay, how about you, Drake?" Nurse Lovington asked.

"Would anyone like to buy some placebos?" Drake asked.

"Vat iz a placebo?" Fritz asked.

"It's a pill that does nothing," Drake said.

"Vy vood anyone vant to buy a pill dat doez nothsing?" Fritz asked.

"Are you taking any medication for your OCD?" Drake asked.

"Ja," Fritz said.

"Does it work?" Drake asked.

"Ja, it helpz, but it doez give me ztomach crampz," Fritz said.

"Well, there you go. The placebo doesn't give you cramps. You need to take a placebo so it will not give you cramps. It also doesn't give you headaches, diarrhea, dry mouth, lightheadedness, nausea or any type of allergic reaction," Drake said.

"How much are dey?" Fritz asked.

"Twenty dollars each," Drake said.

A line formed; everyone stood up to buy placebos. No one wanted any of those side effects that Drake mentioned. Nurse Lovington bought one too. She didn't take any pills; she just thought it was better to be safe than sorry.

"That's all the time we have today for sharing," Nurse Lovington said.

Fritz stood up first to leave.

"Sieg Heil," Crazy Bob said.

Fritz looked at Crazy Bob and shook his head as he goose-stepped out of the room.

Drake couldn't believe it; he had sold all of his placebos and held a wad of cash in his hand.

I don't know why I didn't become a paranoid capitalist earlier, he thought.

Chapter 14

Crazy Bob's room was so cramped; there was hardly any room to breathe. Every single patient was there, including Joseph, who was invisible. Being invisible made it hard not to be stepped on, bumped into or squashed, so you had to be careful. They all wanted to find a fart bug in Crazy Bob's room. Crazy Bob promised them monetary compensation; and monetary compensation was like dysentery that you only got once, according to Drake. So everyone agreed it was better to have it once and get it out of the way instead of getting it and having it forever.

Crazy Bob was trying to sleep but found it almost impossible because he had people looking under his sheets and under his pillows for fart bugs. They were lifting up his shirt, sticking their fingers in his ears, nose and mouth, not to mention other places, just to find a single fart bug. No sooner had someone checked inside his nose, than someone else come over to double- check and triple-check his nose, just to make sure.

"I can't find a single fart bug anywhere," Potbelly said.

"I know; I've checked everywhere," Drake said.

"There haf to be zum here becauze dis room zmellz of fartz," Fritz said.

"Did you check under your swastika?" Drake asked.

"Don't be a moron; I don't haf any zwastikaz," Fritz said.

Fritz checked underneath the swastika arm band that he was wearing, but there were no fart bugs to be found.

Lester was tiptoeing all about the room. If there were any fart bugs, he wasn't going to scare them away.

"I think this is a Canadian conspiracy; they've obviously done something with all the fart bugs," Lester said.

Abram was writhing on the floor screaming because he remembered the soda machine would not give him a soda even though he paid for it.

Drake went over to shake him.

"Stop that. You need to stay focused; we are trying to find fart bugs. Besides, you're squashing poor Joseph," Drake said.

This made Abram quiet down and get up off the floor.

"I'm sorry, Joseph; I didn't see you there," Abram said.

"I can't find a fart bug here or there. I can't find a fart bug anywhere. There is no fart bug under the bed; there is no fart bug in

Bob's head," Sam said.

Everyone agreed at Sam's wise words; he knew just how to put things. Sam was right; there were no fart bugs anywhere.

That is until Crazy Bob himself woke up and found a fart bug.

"I found it; I found a fart bug," Crazy Bob yelled.

He scooped it up with his hands and put it in a container he had on his dresser.

"There, now there is proof. I will show Nurse Lovington and Dr. Boyd that they are real," Crazy Bob said.

One by one, they all left Crazy Bob's room in disappointment. It looked like none of them would get dysentery now because Crazy Bob was going to get it for himself. He marched into Dr. Boyd's office carrying the jar with the stink bug he captured and presented it to Dr. Boyd.

"There, what do you have to say about that?" Crazy Bob said.

Dr. Boyd took the jar from Crazy Bob's hands and looked at it closely.

"That is not a stink bug, Robert; it's a roach," Dr. Boyd said.

"The correct term is fart bug," Crazy Bob said.

"That is not a fart bug; it's a roach," Dr. Boyd said.

"I lived through the 60s, and I know a roach when I see one; and this is definitely not a roach. How would you even smoke it?" Crazy Bob asked.

"It's not a roach you smoke; it's a cockroach," Dr. Boyd said.

"Why didn't you say cockroach in the first place?" Crazy Bob asked.

"I assumed you knew what I meant," Dr. Boyd said.

"Well, you know what happens when you assume things," Crazy Bob said.

"Yes, I do," Dr. Boyd said.

"What happens?" Crazy Bob asked.

"What do you mean?" Dr. Boyd asked.

"I mean, 'Tell me what happens, because I don't know.' Everyone always says, 'You know what happens when you assume things;' but then they don't tell you. They assume that you know what happens when you assume things, and so they never tell you."

"When you assume things, you make a pair of asses out of both you and me," Dr. Boyd said.

"No wonder people just assume that you know what that saying means. They don't want to tell you because it makes no sense. How do you make a pair of asses out of people? I mean my wife was a damn good knitter, but I doubt she could have made a pair of asses," Crazy Bob said.

"I'm sorry. I'm just informing you about the saying," Dr. Boyd said.

"No need to apologize. I know you didn't teach at Berkley like me, so I wouldn't expect you to see the silliness in that saying. Anyway, you got off-topic," Crazy Bob said.

Dr. Boyd pulled out his phone and typed something in.

"See, look. I've pulled up what a cockroach looks like," Dr. Boyd said.

Crazy Bob looked closely at the picture and read the caption.

"Periplaneta Americana. That doesn't sound like a cockroach to me; it sounds more like a place the Romans conquered," Crazy Bob said.

"That is just its Latin classification," Dr. Boyd said.

He pulled up another picture.

Crazy Bob looked closely at it.

"Periplaneta Americana is an American cockroach, also known as the water bug. How do you know it is not also known as the fart bug, since it seems to have a number of different aliases?" Crazy Bob asked.

Dr. Boyd took his phone back and typed in something else and handed it to Crazy Bob.

"That is a picture of a fart bug. Do you see the difference between the two?" Dr. Boyd asked.

Crazy Bob nodded his head sadly. He was not going to be able to give himself dysentery. He felt even worse when the realization hit him that he had forgotten to write all of this down. Then something occurred to him, and his face brightened.

"Dr. Boyd, I have roaches infesting my room; and they are roaching up the place. Someone needs to do something about this," Crazy Bob said.

Dr. Boyd sighed, "We will look into it, Robert."

Chapter 15

"I'm feeling fine. I haven't felt bi-polarish in a while," Potbelly said.

Dr. Olive only smiled.

Leave it to a bipolar to say he's not feeling bi-polarish, he thought.

"How come you don't write anything I say down?" Potbelly asked.

"I don't need to; I have an excellent memory," Dr. Olive said.

"Crazy Bob says that Dr. Boyd writes things down," Potbelly said.

"Is that so?" Dr. Olive asked.

Dr. Olive had only been on staff for eight years, two years less than Dr. Boyd, who was the senior doctor. Whether it was to see who prescribed the most pills or who had the craziest patient, they were always in competition with each other over something.

Since Dr. Olive had gotten Drake to sell his placebos, he was now leading that competition. Placebos were in high demand.

As far as who had the craziest patient, it was probably Dr. Boyd, since he saw Crazy Bob; and Crazy Bob was the craziest patient around.

"He says it's so he can remember the conversations he's had with his patients," Potbelly said.

"Well, I have a photographic memory and don't need to write things down," Dr. Olive said.

"That must be nice; I wish I had a photographic memory too," Potbelly said.

"I understand that your mother came to visit you last week. How did that go?" Dr. Olive asked.

"We talked about that last week, don't you remember?" Potbelly asked.

"We did? Oh yes, of course; I just wanted to discuss it a second time," Dr. Olive said.

"I think your photographic memory might be out of focus, Dr. Olive," Potbelly said.

"Please continue," Dr. Olive said, ignoring that last comment.

"It went well, you know, as well as can be expected," Potbelly said.

"How do you mean?" Dr. Olive asked.

Dr. Olive looked at the owl clock on his desk. He had a bad habit of constantly checking his clock as if he could make the time go by faster simply by willing the hand to move along.

"She keeps nagging me about getting married. She says it's time I stop sowing my wild oats and settle down and have children," Potbelly said.

"How does that make you feel?" Dr. Olive asked.

"I told her that I've been here thirty-five years and that I haven't yet sowed any wild oats. She thinks I'm just making excuses and that I'm determined to let her die without any grandchildren," Potbelly said.

"What was your response to her?" Dr. Olive said.

"I said I'd see what I could do," Potbelly said.

"Richard, you really need to stand up to her. We've talked about this," Dr. Olive said.

"I know, but she's seventy-five years old; I don't want to break her heart. I'm her only son, and she probably won't live much longer. I don't see anything wrong with giving her a little hope. Do you know what I mean, Dr. Olive?" Potbelly asked.

Dr. Olive was leaning his head back against his chair with his eyes closed.

"Go on, I'm just resting my eyes," Dr. Olive said.

"I was just saying that she probably won't live much longer; and she is suffering from dementia anyway, so a little white lie can't hurt anything," Potbelly said.

Dr. Olive closed his eyes again, but Potbelly continued assuming he was still resting his eyes.

"I had a girlfriend once. Her name was Leslie; she was my high school sweetheart. We planned to get married after high school. I was going to work in her father's steel mill. She died in a car accident a week before we were going to get married. I've just never felt the same about a girl since," Potbelly said.

The alarm on Dr. Olive's clock began to ring. Dr. Olive woke up with a start. He always set the alarm before he saw his patients in case he fell asleep.

"Well, that's fascinating, Richard. That's all the time I have for now. We'll continue where we left off next week," Dr. Olive said.

"Dr. Olive," Potbelly said.

"Yes, what is it, Richard?" Dr. Olive asked.

"I really haven't felt bi-polarish in a while. Crazy Bob is getting out of here the day after tomorrow. I'd really like to go with him," Potbelly said.

Dr. Olive smiled. He had a wide grin like the Cheshire Cat from *Alice in Wonderland*. He seriously doubted Crazy Bob was going anywhere, and he didn't know why Dr. Boyd kept giving him hope.

He gave him the popular doctor answer.

"We'll see."

Chapter 16

"Hey, who is the new patient?" Crazy Bob asked.

"It's Godot; who else?" Potbelly said.

"What? I assumed Lester was lying about the whole thing," Crazy Bob said.

"Well, you know what happens when you assume," Drake said.

"You make a pair of asses out of you and me," Crazy Bob said.

"What are you talking about?" Drake asked.

"When you assume, you make a pair of asses out of you and me," Crazy Bob said.

"That makes no sense," Drake said.

"It's metaphorical," Crazy Bob said.

Crazy Bob scribbled down his conversation so far with Drake in his notebook.

"Ahh, now it makes sense. It made no sense until you said it was metaphorical because metaphors aren't meant to make any sense whatsoever," Drake said.

"I don't see the point of metaphors," Potbelly said.

"The point is to take things that make no sense and make some sense out of them," Drake said.

"Advertising is the rattling of a stick inside of a swill bucket," Crazy Bob said.

"That makes no sense," Drake said.

"It's a metaphor," Crazy Bob said.

"Ahh, now it makes perfect sense," Drake said.

"You know I worked in advertising for a time. We didn't advertise sticks or swill buckets, though. The advertisements I worked on were for men's deodorant," Potbelly said.

"I don't wear deodorant," Crazy Bob said.

"I remember one of the slogans I came up with. 'If you like smelling nice, try Baron deodorant,'" Potbelly said.

"I like that; it's really catchy. It just rolls off the tongue," Crazy Bob said.

"Godot approaching, two o'clock," Drake said.

Crazy Bob looked at his watch.

"It's only a quarter after eleven," Crazy Bob said.

Godot was a lanky man, probably about six feet tall. He was wearing a top hat and a vest with no pants. The only thing he had on were his tighty whities.

"My name is Godot. Lester tells me that you all waited for me, and I just wanted to thank you," Godot said.

Godot held out his hand, and Crazy Bob shook it. Drake shook his hand as well. When Potbelly shook it, it detached right from Godot's arm.

"I thought you had gum disease?" Crazy Bob asked.

"No, I just have your regular garden-variety leprosy, where anything can fall off at any time," Godot said.

"That's a relief; we were worried you had gum disease," Potbelly said.

"If I had gum disease, Nurse Lovington wouldn't have admitted me. I might have contaminated the place," Godot said.

"Did you get leprosy from an armadillo?" Crazy Bob asked.

"No, I spent some time in Mozambique; and that's where I contracted it," Godot said.

"What were you doing in Mozambique?" Potbelly asked.

"I worked for FedEx," Godot said.

"They have FedEx in Mozambique?" Crazy Bob asked.

"They have FedEx's all over the world. I think I got leprosy from one of the packages I delivered," Godot said.

"What happened to your pants?" Drake asked.

"Someone stole them," Godot said.

"Who would want to steal your pants?" Potbelly asked.

"Perhaps someone who has a pants fetish," Godot said.

"If I were a thief, I think I would steal pants," Crazy Bob said.

They all turned to look suspiciously at Crazy Bob.

"I said if I were a thief," Crazy Bob said.

"Would you like to buy a placebo, Godot?" Drake asked.

"What's it for?" Godot asked.

"It's for not getting gum disease or any other disease you can think of. They are twenty dollars each," Drake said.

"Does it cure leprosy?" Godot asked.

"No, it can't cure a disease you've already contracted. It doesn't prevent diseases, but it doesn't cause them either," Drake said.

"I see; I will try one," Godot said.

"I'll buy one too; I don't want to get gum disease," Crazy Bob said.

"I'll buy two of them for double protection," Potbelly said.

They each handed him the money, and Drake reached in his pocket and pulled out the placebos. He gave one to each except for

Potbelly who got two.

"So sit down and tell us a little more about yourself," Drake said.

"Well, my name is Godot, and I'm an absurdist," Godot said.

"What a coincidence; Crazy Bob is an absurdist too," Potbelly said.

"I don't believe in coincidences," Godot said.

"Nor do I; nor does any good absurdist," Crazy Bob said.

"Where does the name Godot come from? Is it a family name?"

"Yes, my father was a Godot and his father and his father before him," Godot said.

"So you're Godot IV?" Potbelly asked.

"I'm the fourth person in my family named Godot, but I'm not called Godot IV. We don't believe in sequences. I come from a long line of Godots and absurdists," Godot said.

"How do you spell your name?" Drake asked.

"It's spelled G-o-d-o-t," Godot said.

"That is an interesting spelling. It's pronounced God-oh but spelled with a silent T," Potbelly said.

"We do believe in silent Ts," Godot said.

"I think all Ts should be silent," Crazy Bob said.

"I don't think they should be in the alphabet at all," Potbelly said.

"We waited a number of days for you; we didn't think you were ever going to show up," Crazy Bob said.

"Most people don't. What are you writing?" Godot asked.

"I like to write down all my conversations, so that I may reference them again at a later point," Crazy Bob said.

"What later point?" Godot asked.

"Probably after I die," Crazy Bob said.

"That's sensible," Godot said.

"It's getting a little difficult; I have so many conversations," Crazy Bob said.

"What you need is a secretary," Godot said.

"What a great idea. Do you know any secretaries?" Crazy Bob asked.

"I've done some secretarial work in my day. If you can write it all down in short hand, I can type them out later for you," Godot said.

"That sounds wonderful; thank you, Godot," Crazy Bob said.

"Here, you'll need this back if you're going to type," Potbelly said.

Potbelly handed Godot back his hand.

"You're welcome; it's the least I can do for you guys for waiting for me," Godot said.

"Well, everyone is waiting on something. Potbelly is waiting to get a book on pot-bellied pigs, Abram is waiting on a drink from the soda machine, and I'm waiting to get out of here the day after next Monday," Crazy Bob said.

"I thought you were getting out of here the day after tomorrow," Potbelly said.

"No, Dr. Boyd pushed it back a few days. He wanted to have one more session with me first," Crazy Bob said.

"I'm happy for you, but I'll miss you. I don't think they could ever replace you here," Potbelly said.

Chapter 17

"How are you feeling today, Lester?" Dr. Olive asked.

"Why do you ask?" Lester asked suspiciously.

"Because I'm your doctor and I'm concerned about your well-being," Dr. Olive said.

"How do I know you are a real doctor?" Lester asked.

Dr. Olive walked over to his wall and grabbed his diploma from John Hopkins University and handed it to him.

"So, this could be a forgery," Lester said.

"You've been seeing me for five years, Lester," Dr. Olive said.

"How do I know you are not a very patient Canadian spy sent here to try and gain my trust?" Lester asked.

Dr. Olive pointed to the lettering stitched on his jacket.

Dr. Olive, MD.

Lester seemed satisfied and just grunted.

"Lester, why do you think you were in the CIA?" Dr. Olive asked.

"I was in the CIA," Lester said.

"Your file indicates you were unemployed for a number of years, and then you were a copier repairman," Dr. Olive said.

"That was just a cover," Lester said.

"Do you know what your diagnosis is?" Dr. Olive asked.

"Borderline personality disorder and liar, liar pants on fire syndrome," Lester said.

"That is correct," Dr. Olive said.

"I'm beginning to think that is not a real diagnosis; I think you made that up," Lester said.

"I assure you it is a diagnosis; you can look it up in the DSM-5," Dr. Olive said.

"No, I don't like their music," Lester said.

"I hear that you've been telling Crazy Bob and others not to take their medication," Dr. Olive said.

"Where did you hear that? Let me see that file," Lester said.

Lester tried to grab the file from Dr. Olive.

"It's classified," Dr. Olive said.

"What? It can't be classified; only government documents can be classified," Lester said.

"I just meant I don't want you looking at the file; it is for my own personal use," Dr. Olive said.

"Yes, I did tell Crazy Bob and others not to take their medications because I suspect Canadian covert ops are infiltrating the drug companies," Lester said.

"What have you got against Canada anyway?" Dr. Olive asked.

"Nickelback for one thing," Lester said.

"I see. Last time we were discussing your first three marriages; let's delve a little further this time," Dr. Olive said.

"What's to discuss? My first three wives were ungrateful whores," Lester said.

"Let's start with your first wife, Tracey. What do you think went wrong in that relationship?" Dr. Olive said.

"Tracey was always on me about something, whether it was about getting a job, stop telling lies or not doing enough chores around the house," Lester said.

"Were you doing those things?"

"I've had plenty of jobs; I was even once a therapist like yourself," Lester said.

"Is that a lie?" Dr. Olive asked.

"Yes, it is; but I wanted to be a therapist," Lester said.

"Why do you think you felt the need to lie to me just then?" Dr. Olive said.

"I don't know; it's an impulse I can't control. It's like I have Tourette's syndrome. Are you sure I don't have Tourette's syndrome?" Lester asked.

"Don't be ridiculous; there's no such thing as Tourette's syndrome," Dr. Olive said.

"What types of jobs did you have?" Dr. Olive continued.

"We've been over all of this before," Lester said.

"Yes, but we've only skimmed the surface; and I want you to try and be honest, not for my sake but for your own," Dr. Olive said.

"I worked as a copier repairman, waiter, dishwasher, telemarketer, used car salesman and male escort," Lester said.

Dr. Olive raised an eyebrow.

"You never mentioned that you were a male escort before; is that really true?" Dr. Olive said.

"Yes, it was the reason my first wife divorced me," Lester said.

"Why did your second and third wives divorce you?" Dr. Olive asked.

"My second wife, Helen, didn't divorce me; she just left me because she was tired of being broke all the time. And my third wife,

Melinda, divorced me because she found out I was still married to my second wife," Lester said.

"You were a polygamist?" Dr. Olive asked.

"No. I might be a lot of things, Dr. Olive; but I'm not a racist. Fritz is the racist; he thinks I'm a Jew because of my nose. I keep telling him I am Italian, but he doesn't listen to me. Sometimes I think he might be plotting to kill me," Lester said.

"I mean you had more than one wife at the same time?" Dr. Olive asked.

"Oh, yes. You should just say what you mean and not use fancy words," Lester said.

"Sorry. When you say you think Fritz is plotting to kill you, why do you think that?" Dr. Olive said.

"Because he said, 'I am plotting to kill you,'" Lester said.

Lester waited, but Dr. Olive didn't respond because he closed his eyes and started to nod off.

"Dr. Olive, don't you have anything to say about the fact that Fritz is threatening me?" Lester asked.

Dr. Olive opened his eyes with a start.

"Yep, that's messed up," Dr. Olive said.

"Aren't you going to do anything about it?" Lester asked.

"About what?" Dr. Olive said.

"About that Nazi-loving bastard threatening me?" Fritz asked.

"Now, Lester, we were doing so well and then you reverted back to lying. We don't have any Nazis here," Dr. Olive said.

"Are you looney? He wears a swastika," Lester said.

"I don't like the term 'looney;' we don't use that term here," Dr. Olive said.

"The name of our company is Looney Bin Incorporated," Lester said.

"That's just a title; it doesn't mean anything. I prefer you use the term 'reality challenged,'" Dr. Olive said.

"Fritz is reality challenged," Lester said.

"It looks like we are out of time; we'll pick up again next week about why you think Fritz is reality challenged, as you put it," Dr. Olive said.

Just as Lester was leaving, he bumped into Fritz outside the door. Fritz narrowed his eyes at Lester.

"I'm not Jewish, you idiot, I'm Italian; and even if I were Jewish, fascism is so 1945," Lester said.

"Vatch your mouth, Jew," Lester said.

"Fritz, come in and stop bothering Lester," Dr. Olive yelled from inside his office.

Fritz walked into Dr. Olive's office, stood at attention and saluted before he sat down in the chair.

"First things first, Fritz; I need you to stop threatening Lester. We have a no-tolerance policy," Dr. Olive said.

"Vat does *no-tolerance polizy* mean?" Fritz asked.

"It means we don't tolerate anything, whether it is racism or free speech or individuality. We treat all our patients here the same; you are all equally crazy. Do you understand?" Dr. Olive said.

"Jew not tolerate zee racizm," Fritz said.

"Not *Jew* but *you*." Dr. Olive said.

"Das ist vat I zay," Fritz said.

"You said *Jew* instead of *you*," Dr. Olive said.

"I still haf trouble vith engliz pronunziation," Fritz said.

"No more racism, fascism or *ism's*," Dr. Olive said.

"Vat about zvaztikaz?" Fritz asked.

"Swastikas are fine," Dr. Olive said.

"How come Crazy Bob can be into abzurdizm, but I can't be into fazizm?" Fritz asked.

"Because Robert is absurd, so it's quite appropriate for him to be an absurdist," Dr. Olive said.

Fritz crossed his arms and pouted.

"You're a puzzle to me. You deny being a Nazi, but you go around wearing swastikas and making anti-Semitic remarks," Dr. Olive said.

"I am, how do you zay, zee complex man," Fritz said.

"Alright, fair enough," Dr. Olive said.

"Vell ,vat do jew vant to talk aboutz?" Fritz asked.

"I want to talk about Jew—I mean you," Dr. Olive said.

"Mein vater called me yesterday," Fritz said.

"Where again is your father from?" Dr. Olive asked.

"He iz from ze Netherlandz, vich iz vere I'm from," Fritz said.

"Your grandfather was from Germany?" Dr. Olive asked.

"Ja, das ist right," Fritz said.

"Your grandfather was an SS officer?" Dr. Olive asked.

"Ja, he left Germany after zee var," Fritz said.

"You spent a lot of time with your grandfather?" Dr. Olive asked.

"Ja, ve zpent a lot of time togezer. He gave me mein very first zwaztika und pozter of the Furher giving hiz zpeech at Nuremburg," Fritz said.

"I see, so you were indoctrinated at a very young age?" Dr. Olive asked.

"Vat dis mean 'indoctrinated'?" Fritz asked.

"It means of or having the ability to indoctrinate," Dr. Olive said.

"Um...ja, I guezz," Fritz said.

"What did you and your father talk about on the phone?" Dr. Olive asked.

"He vanted to know ven I wuz coming home," Fritz said.

"Not until you are rehabilitated," Dr. Olive said.

"Again vat doez dis vord mean 'rehabilitated'?" Fritz asked.

"It means never," Dr. Olive said.

"He alzo told me meine mutter ist very zick," Fritz said.

"What's wrong with your mother?" Dr. Olive asked.

"Ze haz liver cancer," Fritz said.

"I'm sorry to hear that, Fritz. We'll see if we can arrange a trip for you to see her in the Neverlands," Dr. Olive said.

"Netherlandz," Fritz corrected.

"Tomato, tomahto," Dr. Olive said.

"Nein, zey don't gro tomatoez in zee Netherlandz. It'z a zmall country und very cold," Fritz said.

"What do they grow?" Dr. Olive asked.

"Drugz," Fritz said.

"Really? Well, I don't see why we couldn't arrange a trip for you to go to What's It land. I mean your mother is dying, after all. Do you think you could bring back some pot? Our supplies here are running low," Dr. Olive asked.

"Ve huv a zupply of pot here?" Fritz asked.

"We did, but I smoked most of it," Dr. Olive said.

"Vell, I guezz I could getz zum from meine mutter; ze zmokez zum to help with ze pain," Fritz said.

"That's great, Fritz. We'll arrange a trip to Nevermind so you can bring back some pot," Dr. Olive said.

"Und to zee meine mutter," Fritz reminded him.

"That is what I meant to say," Dr. Olive said.

Chapter 18

"Have you had any more dreams about your wife?" Dr. Boyd asked.

Bob wrote down the question in his notebook.

"What are you writing?" Dr. Boyd asked.

"I'm writing down all of my conversations, just like you do," Crazy Bob said.

"Why are you doing that?" Dr. Boyd asked.

"I want to remember them and review them at some point," Crazy Bob said.

"It sounds time-consuming," Dr. Boyd said.

"It is, but I think observation is the key to self-awareness," Crazy Bob said.

"That's very astute of you, Robert. So, have you had any more dreams about your wife?" Dr. Boyd asked.

"Yes, it was a similar dream as last time. Only instead of my wife knitting me a sweater, she was knitting a pair of asses," Crazy Bob said.

"Why was she knitting a pair of asses?" Dr. Boyd asked.

"I must have assumed something," Crazy Bob said.

"Bob, do you remember what happened to your wife?"

"She was murdered," Crazy Bob said.

"Do you remember who murdered her?" Dr. Boyd asked.

"Our dog Spot," Crazy Bob said.

"You said in the police report that the dog told you to kill your wife, and the dog's name was Fido," Dr. Boyd asked.

"I don't remember the dog's name anymore," Crazy Bob said.

"You never owned a dog; you're allergic to dog hair," Dr. Boyd said.

"Now that I think about it; it was our cat Tabby that told me to kill my wife and to kill the dog Fido," Crazy Bob said.

"I see. Why do you think the cat would want you to kill anyone?" Dr. Boyd asked.

"I don't know why she told me to kill my wife, but I would think the dog is an obvious one," Crazy Bob said.

"You do remember why you are here then?" Dr. Boyd asked.

"Yes, for killing my wife," Crazy Bob said.

"Good, this is progress. You usually don't remember what happened to her, and you think she is still at home waiting for you," Dr. Boyd said.

"You know I was supposed to get out of here the day before yesterday," Crazy Bob said.

"Yes, I know," Dr. Boyd said.

"So can I go ahead and leave today?" Crazy Bob asked.

"No, the day before yesterday has already passed. If you would have remembered then, you could have left; but since you forgot, you can't go back to the day after yesterday and leave," Dr. Boyd said.

"I see," Crazy Bob said.

Crazy Bob hung his balding head down in sadness. He wiped a tear away from the corner of his eye using his flannel shirt.

"The good news is that you can get out of here the day after one month from now," Dr. Boyd said.

Crazy Bob perked up.

"Really, that's not long at all," Crazy Bob said.

"Also, I'm going to triple your medication," Dr. Boyd said.

"Okay, why so much, though?" Crazy Bob asked.

"Dr. Olive doubled all his patients' medications, so I'm going to triple mine. Let's see what he has to say about that," Dr. Boyd said.

"Okay, I guess triple my dosage won't hurt anything except maybe cause me to have a seizure, stroke or stop my heart," Crazy Bob said.

"By the way, Nurse Lovington checked your room and found several cockroaches. It seems you left some half-eaten peanut butter crackers under your bed, which must have been attracting them," Dr. Boyd said.

Crazy Bob chuckled.

"Well, vindicated at last."

Godot knocked on the door.

"Come in, Godot. Our time is up, Robert," Dr. Boyd said.

Godot walked in; he was still only wearing a top hat, vest and his underwear. His pants must still be on the loose somewhere out there waiting to be found and returned to its owner.

"I love your top hat; I would like to get one of those. Where did you get yours?" Crazy Bob asked.

"My dead uncle gave it to me," Godot said.

"He gave it to you when he was alive, or did he bequeath it to you?" Crazy Bob asked.

"He was wearing it at the wake. I took it off his head and put it on my head and have been wearing it ever since," Godot said.

"So you stole it off his head under the assumption that he was

69

going to bequeath it to you at some point?" Crazy Bob asked.

"Exactly, I always take things under the assumption that they will be bequeathed to me at a later date," Godot said.

"What if you die before the person that you assumed was going to bequeath something to you? What happens to the item they bequeathed prematurely?" Crazy Bob asks.

"They can take back the item because I re-bequeath it," Godot said.

"Godot, we need to get started. I'm on a tight schedule."

"Robert, I'll see you next week, okay?" Dr. Boyd said.

Crazy Bob left and Godot sat down.

"The chair is still warm. It feels nice on my bum," Godot commented.

"Yes, well about that. Godot, you really need to start wearing clothes. We have a dress code here at Looney Bin Incorporated. It's in the employee hand book," Dr. Boyd said.

"What is the policy?" Godot said.

"That you wear clothes," Dr. Boyd said.

"What is Looney Bin Incorporated?" Godot asked.

"This facility is Looney Bin Incorporated. It's where you work," Dr. Boyd said.

"I don't remember applying for any jobs," Godot said.

"You don't apply here; you are sent here," Dr. Boyd said.

"Like a package or a piece of mail?" Godot asked.

"Precisely," Dr. Boyd said.

"I know a lot about packages; I use to work for FedEx," Godot said.

"Is that so? Did you enjoy working there?" Dr. Boyd said.

"I did until I got leprosy. It's hard to deliver packages when your limbs keep falling off. I assumed this place was a leper colony," Godot said.

"Why would you assume that?" Dr. Boyd said.

"Because I'm a leper," Godot said.

"We don't like to assign names around here or define people with finite terms," Dr. Boyd said.

"Is that why there is no sign above the door for the bathroom?" Godot said.

"That's correct. We don't call it the bathroom; we call it the artistic expression room," Dr. Boyd said.

"I think I should be in a leper colony and not a looney bin. I don't fit in here," Godot said.

"I think you are a perfect fit here. You just need to put some clothes on," Dr. Boyd said.

"Someone has stolen my clothes," Godot said.

"Who would want to steal your clothes?" Dr. Boyd said.

"Perhaps I bequeathed them to someone," Godot said.

"Tell me a little bit about your life. I don't have a lot of information about you in my file," Dr. Boyd said.

"I come from the Midwest, and I am an absurdist like Crazy Bob," Godot said.

"Oh no, not another one of those," Dr. Boyd said.

"What was that?" Godot asked.

"I said, 'Gee, that's nice,'" Dr. Boyd said.

"No, you didn't," Godot said.

"Go on with what you were saying," Dr. Boyd said.

"I suppose you believe in God?" Godot asked.

"Yes, I do believe in God," Dr. Boyd said.

"I don't; if God wanted me to believe in him, he wouldn't have made me an absurdist," Godot said.

"God didn't make you anything," Dr. Boyd said.

"Well, he sure as hell didn't make me any clothes," Godot said.

"What kind of childhood did you have?" Dr. Boyd asked.

"I grew up in a chocolate factory," Godot said.

"You must have had a delightful childhood," Dr. Boyd said.

"No, I didn't. When I was a kid, my parents painted me green and told everyone I was an Oompa Loompa. It was good for business but bad for my self- esteem. By the time I was twelve, I was already six feet tall; and they were still telling people I was an Oompa Loompa," Godot said.

Dr. Boyd put his hand to his mouth to muffle a snicker.

"How very tragic that sounds," Dr. Boyd said.

"It was; they painted my brothers and sisters as well. My parents were wealthy, but they never bought us anything or cooked us a proper dinner. We just ate chocolate all the time, which is probably why we are all diabetics," Godot said.

"Were you married?" Dr. Boyd asked.

"I was married once. I'm still wearing my wedding clothes, as a matter of fact," Godot said.

"You got married in your underwear and a top hat?" Dr. Boyd asked.

"Yes, I didn't have anything else," Godot said.

"How long ago were you married?" Dr. Boyd asked.

"About ten years ago," Godot said.

"You're still wearing the same underwear?" Dr. Boyd asked.

"Well, don't look so scandalous; they've been washed a few times since then. I'm not a savage, you know," Godot said.

"I see. To be honest, Godot, I'm really baffled as to what is wrong with you," Dr. Boyd said.

"Why should there be anything wrong with me—I mean, other than the leprosy, that is?" Godot asked.

"You work at Looney Bin Incorporated, so there must be something wrong with you. You're a bit eccentric, but we already have someone here with that. I tell you what, I'm going to open the DSM-5; and you just point to something you think sounds interesting," Dr. Boyd said.

Dr. Boyd handed Godot the DSM-5 book. Godot opened it up and pointed to the first word he saw in the A section.

"You like anorexia. Okay, that works for me," Dr. Boyd said.

Chapter 19

The usual crowd was sitting at their usual table in the dayroom. The table was so usual to the usual crowd that it had a place marker on it labeled "Usual."

"Lester's nephew Parker came in today. I'm so excited," Potbelly said.

"What's so exciting about that?" Drake asked.

"He's fifteen, and I thought he would know all about the technological advancements with pot-bellied pigs," Potbelly said.

"Did you ask him about it?" Crazy Bob asked.

"Yes, he said he didn't know off the top of his head; but the very next chance he got, he would goggle it," Potbelly said.

"What's a goggle? How do you goggle something?" Crazy Bob asked.

"It must be another technological advancement. You probably put on a pair of goggles, and it tells you all the answers in the universe," Drake said.

"I once had a pair of prescription goggles so I could see all the fish while I was scuba diving. I couldn't see all the fish in the universe, though, just the ones in my field of vision," Potbelly said.

"I don't know; it's probably slang. You know how kids are. Are you sure he didn't say he would toggle it?" Crazy Bob asked.

"I am a hundred percent sure that he said he would goggle it," Potbelly said.

Squeak, squeak, squeak…

Nurse Lovington was approaching their table. She was wearing a new white uniform. It was so clean and white that it created a halo. She looked like an angel, an angel in squeaky shoes.

"Time for everyone's meds," she said.

"Richard and Drake, you get double your meds and, Robert, you get triple," Nurse Lovington said.

Crazy Bob counted to three on his fingers.

"You are correct," Crazy Bob said.

"How come he gets triple?" Potbelly asked.

"Dr. Boyd's orders," she said.

She went to the table where Lester, Sam, Fritz and Joseph were sitting. They were arguing over a game of Candy Land.

"Fritz, you were supposed to go back to the ice cream cone," Lester said.

"Dat vuz not my card; dat vuz Zam's card," Fritz said.

"No, I had red. You see I'm ahead," Sam said.

"Damn it, Joseph, you keep forgetting to move your gingerbread man." Somebody move Joseph's gingerbread man," Lester said.

"Vy can't he move it fur himself?" Fritz asked.

"Because he is invisible, you idiot," Lester said.

"Sorry to interrupt. Sam, you are getting triple your medication now. Dr. Boyd's orders," Nurse Lovington said.

"If you lie, I might die," Sam said.

"Well, I can't be bothered if you die or not. It is the doctor's orders, and we all have to follow orders," Nurse Lovington said.

"Dat's right. I vas only followzing orderz," Fritz said.

"I see; you are right. I will not fight," Sam said.

"Here you go, Fritz."

Nurse Lovington handed Fritz a pill and left one on the table for Joseph, along with the huge pile of his other pills that he hadn't taken.

"Now, Joseph, you don't want to be invisible anymore, do you?" Nurse Lovington asked.

Someone started screaming. It was Abram, and he was wearing a welder's helmet and using a blow torch on the drink machine.

Dr. Boyd ran toward Abram from one end of the dayroom and Dr. Olive from the other with a syringe in each hand. They were both sprinting as fast as they could; it was a race to see who could get to Abram first and plunge a needle in him. It was a close race; and just when it looked like Dr. Boyd might win, Dr. Olive grabbed Nurse Lovington's pill tray and slung it in his direction. A rainbow of pills flew towards Dr. Boyd and landed on the ground all around him. He took one step, and his feet slid out from under him. Dr. Olive leaped into the air over the pills and landed in front of Abram, but not before Dr. Boyd sprung back up with his cat-like reflexes and plunged his syringe into Dr. Olive's ass.

By this time, Abram was completely calm and was in no need of a sedative. He was too busy watching the spectacle.

"Abram, help me get Dr. Olive back to his office; he's not feeling well," Dr. Boyd said.

Abram grabbed Dr. Olive's feet, and Dr. Boyd grabbed his midsection; and they carried him out of the dayroom. Drake followed them as Abram and Dr. Boyd put Dr. Olive in his office chair. He slumped forward on his desk. Dr. Boyd pulled the phone cord out from the phone and tied Dr. Olive to his chair.

"Drake, what are you doing here?" Dr. Boyd asked.

"I have an appointment with Dr. Olive," Drake said.

"Dr. Olive can't see you now; he's taking a nap," Dr. Boyd said.

"No, this is how Dr. Olive usually conducts our sessions; he's just resting his eyes," Drake said.

After Dr. Boyd and Abram left, Drake collapsed in the chair and sighed. His face was anguished as if he was reluctant to broach the subject, but he bravely moved forward.

"I wanted to talk about what I'm doing here. I don't really remember why I'm here. The only thing I remember is my dad getting drunk one night and telling me that I was crazy because I liked to draw faces on eggs and that he was sending me to the looney bin," Drake said.

Dr. Olive snored, and his head slumped forward a little bit which Drake took as a nod.

"My dad never really saw me as much. He put me here when I was eighteen, and then he died the following year. All during that time, I waited for a visit or a letter or even a phone call. He was a heavy drinker, my father; it was the death of him. I don't mean the alcohol killed him literally; it was just a contributing factor. No, he got intoxicated one day and decided to ride his unicycle on a busy street. He was hit by a car and died instantly. My father used to ride the unicycle for the Big Apple Circus. I must have gone to thousands of shows growing up. I had a romance with the bearded lady the summer before I was admitted here. Her name was Tasha; she was from Siberia. She was my first and only love. My father found out, and he put an end to it; he said no son of his was going to love a freak. I was a disappointment to him while he was alive. I wish he could see me now, though; I've become a success at something. I've been making quite a bit of money at selling placebos," Drake said.

Dr. Olive began to drool; the drool hung from his lips but refused to fall.

Drake picked up Dr. Olive's coffee mug that said "#1 Doctor" on it, and written underneath that in a sharpie it said "#2 Dr. Boyd."

He got the coffee mug up to Dr. Olive's mouth just in time to catch the drool before it broke off and fell on the desk.

"I didn't really come here to talk about my dad, though. I've made two thousand dollars selling placebos, and I wanted to purchase some more shares of Looney Bin Inc. like we talked about," Drake said.

Dr. Olive's head shifted over to the other side, so Drake took that as an affirmative.

"No need to get up; just keep resting your eyes. I'll fill out the paperwork," Drake said.

Drake reached into Dr. Olive's desk and pulled out a piece of paper. He grabbed a fountain pen and wrote the following:

Drake Edwards purchased two thousand shares of stock in Looney Bin Incorporated for $2,000.

He picked up the paper and folded it. He reached into his back pocket and pulled out a wad of bills and laid it on the desk in front of Dr. Olive.

"Thanks for always listening to me, Dr. Olive, and for all of your good advice," Drake said.

Drake left Dr. Olive's office. The alarm on the owl clock went off. Dr. Olive awoke with a start. He didn't remember what had happened or why he was tied up; he was still groggy from the sedative. He saw the big wad of bills sitting on his desk. He decided he was dreaming and went back to sleep in the hopes that he could make more money appear.

Chapter 20

Dr. Boyd sighed. He was becoming frustrated; these meetings with Sam were tedious because he had to rhyme everything.

"Sam, I know you like Dr. Seuss and you love his story *Green Eggs and Ham,* but that story is for children," Dr. Boyd said.

"Dr. Seuss wrote many wonderful pages. *Green Eggs and Ham* is a story for all ages," Sam said.

"Yes, but just because we like a story, we can't go around imitating it. We have to live our own lives. You are an adult, and you need to speak as one and have intelligent conversations with people," Dr. Boyd said.

"To speak in rhymes is an art. To speak in rhymes is very smart," Sam said.

"I will admit it does take some ingenuity to rhyme everything, but it can't help you speak to me in specific terms. Your rhyming only conveys broad messages," Dr. Boyd said.

"I can convey anything I wish. I can talk about anything including fish," Sam said.

"Alright, let's talk about fish for a second. Let's talk about barracudas," Dr. Boyd said.

Sam shook his head back and forth vigorously.

"Do you see? We can't talk about any subject. We can't talk about barracudas, because you can't rhyme that word. Do you see the limitations with rhyming?" Dr. Boyd asked.

"I can't talk about it because I don't know a lot about that kind of fish. I don't want to talk about them, and that is my wish," Sam said.

"Come now, you do know some things about barracudas even children know," Dr. Boyd said.

"I know that they are different from the carp. I know their teeth are very sharp," Sam said.

Sam was beaming. He had something to say about barracudas after all.

"That's good, Sam, but I still don't think you are getting my point," Dr. Boyd said.

"The point is that horses eat hay. The point is you can't admit that you are gay," Sam said.

"I am not gay. Where did you get that notion?" Dr. Boyd asked.

Sam pointed to his messenger bag hanging from the coat rack.

"Oh, for Pete's sake. I see Robert has been talking about me. I will tell you what I told him. That is not a purse; it is a messenger bag, which I use to carry my laptop," Dr. Boyd said.

"Some people are loud, some are quiet and some seek fame. The point is that not everyone is the same," Sam said.

Dr. Boyd tried a different line of reasoning.

"You know, there are plenty of other stories and poems that are really good that don't rhyme," Dr. Boyd said.

"That might be true, but I am Sam. Sam I am," Sam said.

"What does that mean?" Dr. Boyd said.

"It means that I like rhyming a lot. It means that I cannot be someone I am not," Sam said.

Dr. Boyd reached inside his desk and pulled out *Oliver Twist* by Charles Dickens. He gave the book to Sam.

"Okay, Sam, you've made some valid points. I brought this from home for you. I would like you to read this book."

Sam started to shake his head in the negative.

"You don't have to stop rhyming for now. I just want you to read this book, and hopefully you will enjoy it. We can talk about it at your next appointment," Dr. Boyd said.

"Dickens was no Dr. Seuss. Don't worry, I will put the book to good use," Sam said.

Chapter 21

Crazy Bob was not being crazy at the moment, which meant he was reading. He was halfway through with *Slaughterhouse Five*. The dayroom door was kept open all the time now, thanks to Charles Dickens. Sam had indeed found a good use for the book that Dr. Boyd had given him; it was being used as a doorstop.

Fritz came up to Crazy Bob and peeked over his shoulder.

"Vat are Jew reading?" Fritz asked.

"I'm reading *Mein Kampf*; do you want to borrow it?" Crazy Bob asked.

"Oh, ja, pleaze," Fritz said.

Crazy Bob handed him the book.

"Diz izn't *Mein Kampf*; diz iz *Zlaughterhouze Five*," Fritz said with disappointment.

"It's *Schlachthof-funf* to you," Crazy Bob said.

Fritz gave the book back to Crazy Bob; he huffed and then goose-stepped away.

"Is that about five slaughterhouses?" Potbelly asked.

"It's about one slaughterhouse," Crazy Bob said.

"Why don't they just call it *Slaughterhouse One* then?" Potbelly asked.

"Because no one would want to read a book about only one slaughterhouse; you have to have at least five of them in order to make it interesting," Crazy Bob said.

"What is the story?" Drake asked.

"I taught this book at Duke University. The main character, Billy Pilgrim, gets caught by the Germans at the Battle of the Bulge," Crazy Bob said.

"My father fought the Battle of the Bulge," Potbelly said.

"Did he die?" Crazy Bob asked.

"No, he didn't die; but he lost that war, because he's still pretty fat," Potbelly said.

"It's mainly a story about how Billy becomes unstuck in time and gets abducted by aliens. He ends up in a zoo on the planet Tralfamadore," Crazy Bob said.

"How do you get unstuck in time?" Drake asked.

"The same way you get stuck in time," Crazy Bob said.

"That makes no sense," Drake said.

"It's a metaphor," Crazy Bob said.

"Now it makes perfect sense," Drake said.

"Does he like Tralfamadore?" Potbelly asked.

"Yeah, because he ends up there with a movie star with big boobs," Crazy Bob said.

"I wish I would be abducted by aliens and end up with a movie star with big boobs," Potbelly said.

"Who wouldn't?" Crazy Bob said.

"I rescued a pot-bellied pig from being slaughtered once," Potbelly said.

"When was this?" Crazy Bob asked.

"When I was in the Peace Corp, we had an assignment in Uganda. A vicious tribe of pygmies captured a pot-bellied pig and were going to cook it. I saved it from the fire by offering the Pygmies twenty American dollars, some Red Sox baseball cards and a Pink Floyd t-shirt. They were very happy, especially with the Pink Floyd t-shirt; they all took turns wearing it. The shirt extended to their ankles since they are only about four feet tall. I stayed a couple of weeks and then had to leave on another assignment. A buddy told me as soon as I left, they roasted that pot-bellied pig," Potbelly said.

"So you didn't really save the pig from being slaughtered," Drake said.

"No, I guess not; it was only a temporary stay of execution. Those short little savages," Potbelly said.

Potbelly started to tear up. Crazy Bob and Drake patted him on the back until he recovered.

Godot came over and handed some papers to Crazy Bob. His one hand had been reattached by Nurse Lovington; but when he handed the papers to Crazy Bob, his other hand fell off. He was still wearing the vest and top hat, but Nurse Lovington had made him put some pants on.

"I typed all your papers up for you," Godot said.

Crazy Bob examined them.

"These are all typed up in shorthand," Crazy Bob said.

"I know, I can't read shorthand," Godot said.

"Yes, but I wrote down my notes in shorthand, so that you could type them up in long hand," Crazy Bob said.

"I don't know shorthand," Godot said.

"I don't know it either. I thought maybe you did and could figure out what I was trying to say," Crazy Bob said.

"So now neither of us understands what it is I wrote," Crazy Bob said.

"I know, it's the perfect system," Godot said.

"By God, you're right," Crazy Bob said, beaming.

Isabella the cook walked into the dayroom carrying egg cartons. She spotted Drake and came bounding over.

"I have to run to the bathroom," Godot said.

"I haven't seen you in the kitchen lately, Drake, so I brought you some eggs," Isabella said.

"Why do you need eggs?" Crazy Bob asked.

"I like to draw faces on the eggs," Drake said.

"What do you do with the eggs after you've finished drawing faces on them?" Godot asked.

"I give them back to Isabella, so she can cook them for our breakfast," Drake said.

"What kind of faces do you give them?" Potbelly asked.

"I draw all kinds. Most of them have happy faces. I even give some hair or glasses or maybe even buck teeth," Drake said.

"But if they're going to get eaten later, shouldn't they all have sad faces?" Godot asked.

Drake thought about that for a minute.

"I guess you're right, but I don't think it would be any fun to draw all sad faces on the eggs," Drake said.

"But it would be sadistic to draw happy faces on the eggs, knowing they were going to get scrambled or boiled alive," Crazy Bob said.

"There is only one solution. You must keep the eggs, that way you can draw any face you want on them because they will be safe," Godot said.

"What about our breakfast?" Drake asked.

"We will just have to forgo eggs for breakfast and eat oatmeal," Potbelly said.

Isabella opened the carton of eggs and passed them out. She put a box of crayons in the middle of the table.

Crazy Bob drew wisps of hair on the side of the egg and gave his egg some glasses.

"Look, it's me," he said.

They all looked at the face that Crazy Bob drew. It was a remarkable self-portrait.

There was a little commotion at the door. Dr. Raven, along with some executives from their advertising department and a camera crew, flooded the room.

Nurse Lovington squeaked in and announced that they were shooting a commercial.

"Why are they making a commercial?" Potbelly asked.

"It's for advertising," Crazy Bob said.

"Advertising what?" Potbelly asked.

"Looney Bin Incorporated," Crazy Bob said.

"What's that?" Potbelly asked.

"That's us," Crazy Bob said.

They were all gathered in the dayroom, ready to make the commercial.

"Is everyone here?" Dr. Raven asked.

"We are still waiting on Godot," Crazy Bob said.

"I don't think we can wait any longer for him; he'll have to be in the next commercial," Dr. Raven said.

"Robert, you speak first; just read the lines on the teleprompter," Dr. Raven said.

Dr. Raven waited, but Crazy Bob didn't budge.

Potbelly nudged him.

"He means you," Potbelly said.

Crazy Bob walked all the way up to the camera.

"You're standing too close; take a few steps back so we can get all of you," the cameraman said.

Crazy Bob took a few steps back and pulled a comb out of his back pocket. He didn't have any hair on the top, but he combed the little wisps he had left growing on the side of his head. He was wearing his flannel shirt and sweating profusely because it was summertime. He looked like Nixon when he was debating Kennedy in the 1960s. He didn't have a handkerchief, so he wiped his face on the sleeve of his shirt. He swatted at an imaginary stink bug and scratched his belly.

"Do you hear voices? Do they tell you to do things like kill the cat or paint the toilet seat red? If so, you might be crazy. Hi, I'm Crazy Bob, and I've been a patient here at Looney Bin Incorporated for thirty-five years; and during that time, I've received topnotch treatment. Here at Looney Bin Incorporated we have the best doctors and nurses available. But don't take my word for it, ask Potbelly, who's also a longtime patient," Crazy Bob said.

The camera panned to Potbelly, who was wearing a head band and a t-shirt with the sleeves cut off.

"Hi, I'm Potbelly and I have bipolar disorder. Do you have

feelings of elation, like you can climb Mount Everest, followed by feelings of depression and you want to blow your head off—" Potbelly paused to chuckle—"Well, then you're just like me; and you belong with us here at Looney Bin Incorporated," Potbelly said.

"Okay, now everyone get in a group; it's time to sing the Looney Bin Incorporated song," the cameraman said.

They all bunched up in a group. Godot walked in just in time to sing the corporate jingle. He was once again not wearing any pants, much to Nurse Lovington's chagrin. Someone must have stolen his pants while he was in the bathroom.

"You're stepping on Joseph's foot, Abram," Lester said.

"Sorry, Joseph, I didn't see you," Abram said.

"Come on out and don't be lazy, if you know you're really crazy. Anxiety and OCD, we want you. Bipolar, schizophrenia and depressives too. So listen to those voices inside your heads, because Looney Bin Inc. has got your meds," sang everyone. Fritz was wearing his swastika and goose-stepping in front of the group and finished off with jazz hands.

Crazy Bob came in late and was off-key. When everyone was already finished, you could hear him sing the last line.

"I think we have a winner; good job, everyone," Dr. Raven said, beaming.

There were refreshments and food laid out in the dayroom, compliments of Looney Bin Incorporated.

Abram was already pouring his third soda, and Potbelly was near tears because of all the poor pigs that must have died to make the ham which Crazy Bob was shoving in his mouth. Nurse Lovington tried to comfort him.

"These aren't pot-bellied pigs; they are regular farm pigs. They just did their duty," Nurse Lovington said.

"I know, they just remind me of the pets I used to have. I really wish I could get a pot-bellied pig," Potbelly said.

"Try the sausage biscuit," Nurse Lovington said.

"Pigs are pets, not food," Potbelly said.

"That's right," Crazy Bob said as he shoved another ham biscuit in his mouth.

Dr. Raven walked up to Crazy Bob.

"Well, how does it feel to be the star of the show?" Dr. Raven asked.

"What show?" Crazy Bob asked.

"It's a figure of speech; I just meant our number one patient here at Looney Bin Incorporated," Dr. Raven said.

Crazy Bob just smiled because he had no idea what he was talking about.

"You know, seeing you in front of the camera gave me a great idea for a reality television show," Dr. Raven said.

"What's the idea?" Crazy Bob asked.

"We get a camera crew in here and film your day-to-day activities and make it into a reality television show," Dr. Raven said.

"But we're crazy; we don't live in reality so wouldn't that make a bad show?" Crazy Bob asked.

"I think it would be a fascinating show. People are always curious as to what crazy people are like and what goes on at a mental institution," Dr. Raven said.

"Isn't that supposed to be confidential?" Crazy Bob asked.

"Nonsense, nothing is confidential when it comes to ratings and money," Dr. Raven said.

"I guess it couldn't hurt to try it out," Crazy Bob said.

"Trust me; it will make a lot of money. I mean just the money in merchandise alone would make a fortune. How'd you like to see your face on a bobble head?" Dr. Raven asked.

Crazy Bob, who had no idea what a bobble head was, nodded his head up and down.

Dr. Raven, who thought he was imitating a bobble head, laughed at the joke. Crazy Bob, not sure why he was laughing, also began to laugh.

"I will talk to my board, and we'll make this happen," Dr. Raven said.

"We'll make it happen," Crazy Bob repeated.

He didn't know what Dr. Raven was talking about, so he thought it was a metaphor.

Chapter 22

Dr. Boyd was leading the contest to see who could see the most patients in a week. Dr. Olive had to see more patients, but he didn't know how he was going to squeeze them in. He decided he would see Dr. Boyd's patients as well. There was no rule that said he couldn't see Dr. Boyd's patients if he wanted to. If Dr. Boyd complained to the board that he was seeing his patients, he would simply say that he was giving them double therapy; and that meant they would be cured in double the amount of time. That would please them; they would think he was a hard worker, a dedicated doctor. He might get a raise; he might even get a transfer to a nicer facility. He had made up his mind; he would start with Crazy Bob and work his way down Dr. Boyd's client list.

He buzzed Nurse Lovington. He could hear the squeak, squeak, squeak of her squeaky shoes in the hallway.

God, why doesn't that woman buy some silent shoes? He thought. She opened his office door and squeaked up to his desk. His office was carpeted, so how she was still able to squeak was a mystery.

"I need a mannequin," Dr. Olive said.

Nurse Lovington didn't even bat an eye.

"Male or female?"

"I need a male with dark hair and glasses. If you can't find one with glasses, don't worry about it," Dr. Olive said.

"Okay, I'll go get one. We keep our mannequins in the supply closet," Nurse Lovington said.

"Why do we have mannequins in the supply closet?" Dr. Olive said.

"I don't know; this is a looney bin, after all," Nurse Lovington said.

"Good point," Dr. Olive said.

After Nurse Lovington left, Dr. Olive checked to see how he was going to work Dr. Boyd's patients into his already busy schedule. It was almost one o'clock, and he was supposed to see Richard at that time. He hated having to spare an hour of his precious time to listen to him blather on about his mother, or worse, pot-bellied pigs.

Nurse Lovington returned, dragging in an unclothed mannequin.

"I'll have to phone the janitor; someone defecated in the supply closet, and it reeks in there," Nurse Lovington said.

"What?" Dr. Olive asked.

"Someone took a crap—"

"I know what defecate means; I was just surprised," Dr. Olive said.

She handed Dr. Olive the mannequin.

"I couldn't find one with glasses, but this one has a dark wig," Nurse Lovington said.

"That's fine; here, put him in my chair. I need to leave; I have an appointment with Robert," Dr. Olive said.

"I thought Crazy Bob was Dr. Boyd's patient?" Nurse Lovington asked.

"Please call all of our patients by their given names; have a little respect for Looney Bin Incorporated, Nurse Lovington. Robert is still Dr. Boyd's patient, but he is also now my patient. All of my patients are my patients, and all of his patients are also now my patients. It's a new program I'm instituting called double secret therapy," Dr. Olive said.

"Sorry, I meant Robert. I understand the double part, but why is it a secret?" Nurse Lovington asked.

"I don't want Dr. Boyd to know about the program because he might get the idea that he should give my patients double secret therapy. I will not allow him to see any of my patients and mess their heads up with all that Freudian nonsense he so vehemently believes in," Dr. Olive said.

"That won't be fair then; all of his patients get double therapy, and yours will only get single therapy," Nurse Lovington said.

"I am going to double my therapy sessions with my patients as well," Dr. Olive said.

"How will you be able to manage all of this?" Nurse Lovington asked.

"Don't worry, Nurse Lovington, I have it all under control," Dr. Olive said.

"Okay, I just don't want you to burn yourself out," Nurse Lovington said.

"I won't; I'm on top of things," Dr. Olive said.

"Okay then, if that's all you need, it's time for me to dispense the patients' medications," Nurse Lovington said.

"That's all; thank you, Nurse Lovington," Dr. Olive said.

He watched her leave and went over to his closet and took out one of the lab coats hanging there. He put the lab coat on the mannequin and rubbed his finger over the stitching of his name.

There, now it's officially me, Dr. Olive thought.

Dr. Olive took a black sharpie from his desk and drew horned-rim glasses on the mannequin to look like his. When he was done, he stood back to admire his handy work.

He's a dead ringer for me, Dr. Olive thought.

Dr. Olive looked at Dr. Mannequin Olive sitting upright in his chair, with his thick, horn-rimmed glasses. He had such an air of dignity about him.

As soon Dr. Olive left, Potbelly walked into his office; it was time for his appointment. Potbelly remained motionless and just stared at the figure in the chair. The man sitting in Dr. Olive's chair had dark hair and black horn-rimmed glasses like Dr. Olive, but something didn't seem right. Potbelly couldn't figure out what was different.

"Have you lost weight, Dr. Olive?"

No response from Dr. Mannequin Olive.

Potbelly hesitated.

"Dr. Olive, is that you?"

Potbelly picked up a pen and walked over to Dr. Mannequin Olive. He poked Dr. Mannequin Olive in the shoulder with the pen. Potbelly examined his coat and noticed it had "Dr. Olive" stitched on it. He breathed a sigh of relief.

"I wasn't sure if it were really you there for a moment. I mean it looks like you, but you seem different somehow. Anyway, I finally told my mother that I would probably never get married or have kids," Potbelly said.

No response from Dr. Mannequin Olive.

"You can go ahead and rest your eyes, Dr. Olive," Potbelly said.

That was already what Dr. Mannequin Olive was doing because behind his horn-rimmed glasses, Dr. Mannequin Olive didn't have any eyes, just two holes.

"She was livid. She said I was no son of hers. I told her I most certainly was, and I pulled my birth certificate out of my pocket to show her. I always carry my birth certificate in my pocket; you never know when one of your parents is going to deny your existence. She asked me why I couldn't be more like my brother Bobby, and I said I didn't have a brother named Bobby. She said I was missing the point, which was that she was going to die without any grandchildren. I told her grandchildren were overrated. She said that I shouldn't talk back to an old lady," Potbelly said.

There was a knock on the door, and Nurse Lovington came in carrying a cup of coffee. She sat it down on Dr. Olive/Dr. Mannequin Olive's desk. She winked at Dr. Mannequin Olive.

"Hi, Richard. Doesn't Dr. Olive look simply dashing today?" Nurse Lovington asked.

"Um, yes. I suppose he does look dashing today," Potbelly said.

Nurse Lovington left the office, preceded by a squeak that made Potbelly wince. He hated the sound of her squeaky shoes; they were like nails on a chalk board.

"I think Nurse Lovington was flirting with you. It must be all that weight you lost," Potbelly said.

Dr. Mannequin Olive stared back with a look of quiet confidence.

"Anyway, I don't want to bore you with the details of my mother's visit. I wanted to move on to pot-bellied pigs. I know you find them just as fascinating as I do," Potbelly said.

Potbelly looked into the face of Dr. Mannequin Olive. There was some transformation that had come over his doctor of eight years. He had a shrewder look about him as if he had gained some worldly wisdom. It wasn't arrogance; it was just the confidence of a person who had all the answers, and this new Dr. Olive had all the answers. Whatever brought on this change, Potbelly decided he liked him even better.

"I know we have talked about this extensively in the past, but I would really like to get a pot-bellied pig. You said there were some health and safety concerns, but I assure you that pot-bellied pigs are actually quite sanitary. I can pay for all its food and vet costs. I think all the other patients would love it; it would be good for morale. There have been lots of studies, and pot-bellied pigs are very therapeutic. Nurse Lovington said she would be willing to pick one out for me at a sanctuary she knows about. What do you say, Doc? Can I get one?" Potbelly asked.

Potbelly waited for Dr. Mannequin Olive to respond. He looked directly into his eyes and searched for an answer in them. After looking into those dark holes for about ten minutes, he decided the answer in them was "yes."

"Oh, thank you, Dr. Olive. You won't regret this; everyone is going to love it," Potbelly said.

The owl clock on Dr. Olive/Dr. Mannequin Olive's desk began

to ring. It rang for a full minute before Potbelly reached for it and shut it off.

The new Dr. Olive isn't about wasting time. He's too busy making important decisions, Potbelly thought.

Chapter 23

"I don't understand. You're saying we have a therapy session now, but I just had a therapy session with Dr. Boyd yesterday. Is he transferring me over to you?" Crazy Bob asked.

"No, Dr. Boyd is still your doctor and will still be having sessions with you, but I will also be having sessions with you and all of his other patients. It is part of a new program I am instituting called double secret therapy," Dr. Olive said.

"Why is it a secret?" Crazy Bob asked.

"It's a secret from Dr. Boyd; I don't want you to say anything to him about it," Dr. Olive said.

Crazy Bob hesitated; he felt uneasy.

"I don't know; I don't like keeping secrets from Dr. Boyd," Crazy Bob said.

"It's a surprise for Dr. Boyd; I'm going to surprise him later on with the news, but first I want to make sure my new program is successful. Just think of it like a surprise party. You don't want Dr. Boyd finding out I had a surprise party planned for him and you told him about it and ruined the whole thing, do you?" Dr. Olive said.

"No, of course not," Crazy Bob said.

"I don't want you to write down our conversations; I know you've been keeping a record of all your conversations, but this needs to stay off the record. Now, shall we begin?" Dr. Olive asked.

"You mean now, but we're in the dayroom. Don't you want to conduct the session in your office?" Crazy Bob asked.

"Here is fine; my office is occupied at the moment," Dr. Olive said.

"Occupied by whom?" Crazy Bob asked.

"Occupied by me," Dr. Olive said.

"I don't understand," Crazy Bob said.

"It's a metaphor," Dr. Olive said.

"Now it's crystal clear," Crazy Bob said.

"I see that you are a self-diagnosed paranoid socialist. How is that working out for you?" Dr. Olive said.

"It's working out very well. Just the other day I got Nurse Lovington to buy a soda for Abram, since he can never get one himself. I believe in a fair and equal society even though I don't trust the people in that society," Crazy Bob said.

"I understand that you are supposed to be released from here the day after the next full moon," Dr. Olive asked.

"Actually, it is the day after that day of the next full moon," Crazy Bob said.

"What are your plans for when you leave?" Dr. Olive asked.

"What plans?" Crazy Bob asked.

"Where are you going to live? How are you going to support yourself, etc.?" Dr. Olive asked.

"I'm going to live at home with my wife Ethel, and I'm going to work as a meteorologist," Crazy Bob said.

"But your wife Ethel is dead, and you're not a meteorologist; you were a teacher," Dr. Olive said.

"I know, but Dr. Boyd said it's good to be optimistic and have goals," Crazy Bob said.

"Why do you want to be a meteorologist?" Dr. Olive asked.

"I've always been fascinated with meteors," Crazy Bob said.

"The study of meteors is called meteoritic," Dr. Olive said.

"Oh, then what's a meteorologist do?" Crazy Bob asked.

"They study weather," Dr. Olive said.

"Oh, that sounds boring," Crazy Bob said.

"Maybe you would like something more interesting like cosmology," Dr. Olive said.

"Why would I want to study makeup? My wife might get a kick out of it, though," Crazy Bob said.

"Your wife is dead," Dr. Olive said.

"I'm trying to be optimistic like Dr. Boyd told me," Crazy Bob said.

"Cosmology is the study of the origin, evolution and fate of the universe," Dr. Olive said.

"That sounds depressing; I think I would rather study makeup," Crazy Bob said.

"Well, it sounds like you have formulated a solid plan. It looks like our time is up," Dr. Olive said.

"But we've only been talking a few minutes," Crazy Bob said.

"Brevity is also part of my new program," Dr. Olive said.

"So, it's double secret brief therapy?" Crazy Bob asked.

"That's correct, Robert," Dr. Olive said.

"Thank you for my double therapy, Dr. Olive; I already feel twice as better," Crazy Bob said.

Dr. Olive smiled with satisfaction.

"You're welcome, Robert."

As Dr. Olive was leaving the dayroom, he bumped into Potbelly.

"Hello, Dr. Olive. How did you get here so quickly? I just left your office," Potbelly asked.

"I'm a very busy guy; I have to be quick on my feet," Dr. Olive said.

Potbelly studied Dr. Olive closely.

"Did you gain a bunch of weight since I last saw you?" Potbelly asked.

"Not a pound," Dr. Olive said.

There was something dramatically different about this Dr. Olive. He didn't seem as confident as the Dr. Olive he just spoke with, the one who had all the answers. As a matter of fact, this Dr. Olive didn't seem so sure of himself at all.

"Thank you for allowing me to get a pot-bellied pig, Dr. Olive," Potbelly said.

"You're wel—wait. What?" Dr. Olive asked.

"I said, 'Thank you for agreeing to let me have a pot-bellied pig,'" Potbelly said.

"I never agreed to let you have a pot-bellied pig," Dr. Olive said.

"Yes you did, back in your office," Potbelly said.

Dr. Olive had no idea what Potbelly was talking about, and then he remembered that Potbelly just had a session with the other Dr. Olive.

"Did he actually say that you could have a pot-bellied pig?" Dr. Olive asked.

"Why are you referring to yourself in the third person, Dr. Olive?" Potbelly asked.

"I meant, did I actually say you could have a pot-bellied pig?" Dr. Olive asked.

"Not in so many words; it was inferred," Potbelly said.

"Well, I changed my mind. I don't think it's a good idea," Dr. Olive said.

Potbelly was devastated. It was the only thing in this world that he wanted. He couldn't understand how Dr. Olive could change his mind so quickly. One minute he was telling him that he could have a pot-bellied pig, and the next he was saying he couldn't. One minute he was wise and confident, and the next he was not. One minute he'd lost weight, and in the next minute he'd put weight back on.

I think Dr. Olive is bipolar like me, and right now he is on the other pole. I don't like this Dr. Olive at all, Potbelly thought.

His thoughts were interrupted by a scream. Abram was at it again. Potbelly knew how he felt; he felt like screaming too. In fact, he went in to the break room and lay down beside Abram, who was kicking his arms and legs like a child having a tantrum.

Abram was startled momentarily by Potbelly's scream, and then he smiled; he finally had someone on his side. Crazy Bob and Drake came in to see who else was screaming.

"Why are you screaming, Potbelly?" Drake asked.

"I want a pot-bellied pig," Potbelly said.

Drake and Crazy Bob got down on the floor too and started to scream.

"This feels good," Crazy Bob said.

"I know, it really works the tension out," Drake said.

Dr. Olive walked in with his syringe, not expecting there to be a crowd of screamers. He didn't have enough sedative for all of them, so he got down on the floor and began to scream too.

Chapter 24

"Damn that Dr. Olive. He's got Drake selling placebos, and they are selling like hot cakes. He's prescribing way more pills than me," Dr. Boyd said.

"Yes, all the patients love them because they don't give them nausea or dry mouth or high blood pressure or gum disease," Nurse Lovington said.

"Gum disease?" Dr. Boyd asked.

"It makes your teeth fall out," Nurse Lovington said.

"I know that; I meant why are the patients worried about gum disease?" Dr. Boyd asked.

"Probably something that Crazy Bob came up with," Nurse Lovington said.

"I can't let Dr. Olive surpass me. Nurse Lovington, I want you to start selling placebos immediately," Dr. Boyd said.

"But Drake is already selling them; won't we flood the marketplace?" Nurse Lovington asked.

"We'll make our placebos different; what color are Drake's placebos?" Dr. Boyd asked.

"They are blue," Nurse Lovington said.

"We'll make ours plaid," Dr. Boyd said.

"Okay, I guess I can. I don't really have any sales experience, though," Nurse Lovington said.

"Neither did Drake before he started. This is America, Nurse Lovington; you can do or be anything you want. You could even be president of Looney Bin Incorporated one day," Dr. Boyd said.

"Do you really think so?" Nurse Lovington asked.

"Sure, why not? I'll order the placebos, and then you start selling them ASAP," Dr. Boyd said.

Potbelly burst into the office; he was out of breath.

"Joseph's dead," Potbelly said.

"How do you know Joseph's dead?" Dr. Boyd asked.

"He dropped to the floor and didn't get back up. I checked, but I don't hear a pulse," Potbelly said.

"Where is he?" Nurse Lovington said.

"He's in the dayroom," Potbelly said.

Potbelly, Nurse Lovington and Dr. Boyd ran to the dayroom.

"Where is he? I can't see him," Dr. Boyd asked.

"That's because he's invisible," Potbelly said.

Potbelly pointed to the floor where Joseph was lying.

Dr. Boyd reached down to feel where he thought Joseph's pulse ought to be. He put his head down close to Joseph's chest and listened.

"He's not breathing. Nurse Lovington, call 911," Dr. Boyd said.

Abram thrust himself on the floor like he was having a tantrum and began screaming.

"I want my soda; why can't I have my soda?"

Dr. Boyd reached into his lab coat, but he was out of syringes. Crazy Bob took hold of the situation. He ran over to Abram and started shaking him.

"What's wrong with you? This is no time to think about your blasted soda. Joseph is dead."

Abram quieted down and began to sniffle.

Lester was tiptoeing around the body.

"This was obviously done by the Canadians; it was an assassination," Lester said.

Everyone gasped, except for Joseph, who was invisible and dead.

"Why would anyone want to assassinate Joseph?" Dr. Boyd asked.

"Come on, Doc, an invisible man. He'd be the best damn secret agent the world has ever seen. They were probably trying to turn him into a double agent, and he refused," Lester said.

"I guess he really is dead," Nurse Lovington said.

They all waited quietly for the ambulance to arrive, even though it was already too late for poor Joseph.

When the paramedics arrived, there seemed to be some confusion about where the body was.

"He's right there by the sofa chair," Potbelly pointed.

"No, he's lying by Crazy Bob's feet," Lester said.

"No, he's sitting in the sofa chair," Crazy Bob said.

Nurse Lovington finally sorted out the confusion.

"Here he is; he's right here by the magazine table," she said.

The paramedics walked over and lifted Joseph's limp and invisible body and put him on the stretcher.

"Poor Joseph," Abram wailed.

"Someone should notify Joseph's family," Potbelly said.

"Notify them about what?" Crazy Bob asked.

"About Joseph being dead," Potbelly said.

"Oh, right," Crazy Bob said.

"I don't know if he even had any family; he was very tight-lipped on that subject," Nurse Lovington said.

"He was invisible; how do you know if he had tight lips or not?" Crazy Bob asked.

"Tight lips sink ships; maybe that's why he died," Potbelly said.

"I meant he never spoke about them," Nurse Lovington said.

"He really didn't talk much at all; you would think invisible people would be more talkative to make up for the fact that they can't be seen," Drake said.

"He was not heard or seen, just like my dog Fido," Crazy Bob said.

"It's just not fair," Abram wailed.

Crazy Bob patted him on the back.

"There, there, I know he was a young man. It really isn't fair," Crazy Bob said.

"No, it's just not fair that Joseph can up and die if he wants, and I can't get a soda," Abram said.

Chapter 25

All of the staff and patients were gathered in the dayroom for a memorial service for Joseph. Everyone had on a suit and tie, except for Nurse Lovington, Godot and Fritz. Nurse Lovington was wearing a crisp white uniform with new shoes that somehow were even squeakier than the last pair. She came in while Potbelly was saying a few short words about Joseph which no one even heard over the squeaks. Godot was once again wearing just a vest, top hat and tighty whities. Fritz was wearing an SS uniform that had been newly starched. He had even ironed his swastika for the occasion.

Drake took an egg from his pocket.

"Why do you have an egg in your pocket?" Crazy Bob asked.

"I drew Joseph's face on it," Drake said.

Drake handed Crazy Bob the egg.

"I don't see a face on the egg," Crazy Bob said.

"I didn't know what his face looked like," Drake said.

Joseph was cremated; the funeral home gave Looney Bin Incorporated a discount since he was invisible. His ashes were put on top of the dayroom coffee table in an urn. Again, the funeral home offered them a discount– since he was still invisible and required little room.

"Would anyone else like to say anything about Joseph?" Dr. Boyd asked.

Sam raised his hand.

"Joseph is dead. Yes, that is what I said. You couldn't see him, but you knew he was there. He could have had brown, blonde or even blue hair."

Everyone nodded their heads; it was indeed true that Joseph was dead and that he could have had blue hair, for all they knew. His cause of death was unknown so they all assumed that Potbelly was probably right, that he had died of tight lips, either that or he was assassinated by the Canadians as Lester suggested.

"Blonde or brown we all agree; Joseph, we hardly knew ye," Sam said.

Sam's words were moving; there wasn't a dry eye in the room.

"Although Joseph refused to take his medication, he was by far the easiest patient I ever had. He never complained; and when the time came, he died without raising a fuss. Joseph will really be missed," Dr. Boyd said.

Drake raised his hand to speak.

"I remember the time when I first met Joseph. I couldn't see him, but he seemed like a nice fellow. Once I accidentally bumped into Joseph and I said, 'Excuse me.' Those were good times. He has left a big hole in all of our hearts."

Fritz raised his hand in the form of a *sieg heil* salute.

"Jozef vaz a gut man. Der Fuhrer okay wid invizible men unlezz dey Jewish invizible men den he haf zmall problem. Not dat I am a Nazi or anyding," Fritz said.

Abram raised his hand to speak.

"I just wanted to say that I didn't know Joseph very well, but I would have shared a soda with him if the drink machine had ever given me one."

Lester wanted to say his piece as well.

"I had an invisible friend once, when I was growing up like Joseph; his name was Max. He was my best and only friend, until my parents said they wished I could be more like Max. We are no longer friends, and I haven't spoken to him to this day," Lester said.

Nurse Lovington squeaked to the front of the room.

"Joseph was a good soul; he never had an unkind word to say about anyone. He didn't have any family so there was no one to contact about his demise; but as far as I'm concerned, we were his family. Also, after the service, if anyone wants to buy a placebo, let me know. I'm selling paisley placebos for $20 apiece. They help prevent tight lips," Nurse Lovington said.

This made Drake, who was sitting by the coffee table, jump up to protest; and as he did, he bumped the coffee table with his knee, tipping over Joseph's invisible ashes.

"Nurse Lovington, you can't sell placebos. I'm selling them; and if you sell them too, you'll cut into my profits," Drake said.

"Never mind that now; you just knocked over poor Joseph's ashes. Go grab a broom and dustpan from the kitchen closet," Nurse Lovington said.

Drake stomped into the kitchen to retrieve the dust pan and broom.

This is the best thing that has ever happened to me; and if she's selling them too, I won't be able to make as much money and buy more stock in Looney Bin Incorporated, he thought. Drake returned to the dayroom. The urn had been turned upright again, and Drake swept around the coffee table. He swept up what he thought was at least most of Joseph's ashes along with dirt, a penny, a gum wrapper and a dead roach. He emptied the contents of the dustpan back in the urn.

Nurse Lovington had already begun selling her paisley placebos.

"I would like to buy a paisley placebo. I don't want to die from tight lips like Joseph," Lester said.

"They are $20 apiece," Nurse Lovington said.

Nurse Lovington took Lester's money and counted it.

"This is only $15.40; you still owe another $4.60," Nurse Lovington said.

"I gave you the equivalent of $20," Lester said.

"I don't understand," Nurse Lovington said.

"No, it's a fact. Women earn on average 77 cents per every dollar a man earns who does the exact same job. Therefore, what I paid you was correct," Lester said.

"Correct according to whom?" Nurse Lovington asked.

"According to *Time* magazine," Lester said.

He pointed to the *Time* magazine on the magazine rack.

Nurse Lovington picked it up and turned to page 32 and looked at the article titled "Women in a Man's World."

"Women earn on average 77 cents for every dollar that men earn for doing the same job," Nurse Lovington read.

"You see, Nurse Lovington. I'd like to give you $20, but I can't break the law of economics," Lester said.

Nurse Lovington was irate. She stormed over to where Dr. Boyd was standing and handed him the bag of placebos.

"You sell them. I refuse to work for slave wages anymore," she said.

Drake smiled with satisfaction. He was back in business.

Thank God for the law of economics, he thought.

Chapter 26

Drake purchased more shares of stock in Looney Bin Inc. As a shareholder he was entitled to a quarterly report. It summed up the company's financial performance within the quarter. Insanity was up by 22% compared to last quarter; the company was doing very well. Drake looked at the colorful pie chart. It was broken up into schizophrenia, borderline personality disorder, bipolar disorder I & II, major depressive disorder, obsessive compulsive disorder and other.

Drake headed into Dr. Olive's office for their appointment. He was about to knock when Dr. Olive burst through the door, nearly knocking Drake over.

"I'm ready for our appointment, Doc," Drake said.

"I can't right now; I'm on my way to another appointment," Dr. Olive said.

"Should I come back later then?" Drake asked.

"Don't be silly; I'll still see you," Dr. Olive said.

"How can you see me, though? You just said you have to go to another appointment," Drake asked.

"Just go on in and sit down; I will be at my desk," Dr. Olive said.

"I don't understand how you will be at your desk when you are standing right here," Drake said.

"Do you know the saying you can't be in two places at once?" Dr. Olive asked.

"Yes," Drake said.

"Well, I can," Dr. Olive said.

"But the laws of physics—"

"It's a metaphor," Dr. Olive said.

"I see," Drake said.

Dr. Olive pushed past him and sprinted out of sight.

Drake went in the office; and, sure enough, just as Dr. Olive said, there sitting at his desk was Dr. Olive. He looked different, though; he looked more poised and better groomed, but his hairpiece was slightly askew.

"I didn't know you wore a hairpiece, Dr. Olive," Drake said.

No response from Dr. Mannequin Olive; he just stared ahead with his cool demeanor.

"I like being a paranoid capitalist; I think it's working out well for me," Drake said.

Dr. Mannequin Olive didn't respond.

Dr. Olive must be trying a new therapeutic technique, Drake thought.

"I wanted to let you know that I am still drawing faces on eggs, but I am keeping them in my room now. I've got them all displayed on my dresser; you should come by and see them sometime. A few were done by Crazy Bob, Godot, Isabella and Potbelly.

Dr. Mannequin Olive with his hairpiece askew didn't respond; he just looked at Drake calmly. Since he didn't reply, Drake plowed ahead.

"It's just that I don't have any family and I was never able to hold down a job, so my new job as a salesman has made me into a new man. I've just never been able to figure out who I am and what I was meant to do until now."

Drake paused to work up the courage to ask his next question.

"I was wondering if I could expand my operation. Lots of people can use placebos, not just people with mental health disorders. I guess what I'm trying to ask is, 'Can I start my own business?' Crazy Bob and Potbelly said they would help me set it up online as soon as we figured out how to use the interwebs thingamabob," Drake said.

Dr. Mannequin Olive's mouth was saying nothing, but there was just something about his eyes; they said, "Yes, sure, anything you want."

"Thank you, Dr. Olive; you won't regret this. You don't even have to be involved. I can order the placebos myself; I don't need a doctor's prescription," Drake said.

Drake hopped up and grasped Dr. Mannequin Olive's hand and shook it vigorously. The force of the handshake knocked his hairpiece off.

"Oh, let me get that for you, Doc. You know, you have a firm handshake."

Drake picked up the hairpiece and put it back on Dr. Mannequin Olive, but he put it on backwards.

"I think this is the best session we have ever had. I like your new silent technique; letting the patient do all the talking is really an ingenious idea. It helps me figure it out for myself without you working everything out for me. I'm going to go ahead and go now. I don't even need the whole hour; I feel like a million bucks," Drake said.

Drake dashed out of the office on cloud nine, and Dr. Mannequin Olive was on a role.

Chapter 27

Virgil from solitary confinement was out and back in the general population. He had been in solitary confinement a long time and was finding it hard to socialize. It was circle time, and he took a seat in the farthest corner. They didn't sit in a circle; it was more of an ellipse so technically it could be called ellipse time.

"I think I should be allowed to have a pot-bellied pig," Potbelly said.

"Here ve go again vith the pot-belly pigz," Fritz said.

"Fritz, how many times have I told you to stop interrupting people at circle time?" Nurse Lovington said.

"Approximately vun hundret and dirty-zix timez," Fritz said.

"That is exactly correct; now let Richard finish," Nurse Lovington said.

"Who's Richard?" Crazy Bob asked.

"You are. No, wait, you're Robert. I think Richard might be dead," Drake said.

"Anyway, if I had a pot-bellied pig, I could bring him out during circle time; and we could pass him around and pet him. They are really good therapy. I mean after a couple of weeks, you'd probably all be cured of your mental illnesses," Potbelly said.

"I want to be well. Pot-bellied pigs are swell," Sam said.

"It's not really up to me, though, Richard. If you want a pot-bellied pig, you'll have to ask Dr. Olive," Nurse Lovington said.

"Wait, who is a pot-bellied pig?" Crazy Bob asked.

"I think it's that used car salesmen you see on TV all the time. The one who says you can buy a car with no money down even if you have no credit or bad credit," Drake said.

"So he sells free cars? Must be damn hard to make a living," Crazy Bob said.

"Yeah, very hard to get rich selling free cars," Drake said.

"I asked Dr. Olive and one minute he said I could, and the next he said I couldn't," Potbelly said.

"I tell you what, Richard. I'll ask Dr. Olive myself and get a firm answer from him," Nurse Lovington said.

"Thank you, Nurse Lovington. I don't know what's been going on with Dr. Olive lately. He seems like a different person from one minute to the next," Potbelly said.

"Well, it's a doctor's prerogative to change his mind," Crazy Bob said.

"It's not a doctor's prerogative; it's a woman's," Nurse Lovington said.

"A woman doesn't have a prerogative; she has a vagina," Crazy Bob said.

"No, a prerogative means a right to do something," Nurse Lovington said.

"I think Nurse Lovington wants to change her vagina," Crazy Bob said.

"How do you do that?" Drake asked.

"You need a doctor like I said originally," Crazy Bob said.

"Who would like to talk next? Virgil, would you like to say something to the group?" Nurse Lovington asked.

Everyone turned at once to look at Virgil. Virgil jumped up and ran for the door. He turned the handle, but it was locked. He looked around, panic-stricken, and bolted toward the window. He tried to raise the window, but it was painted shut. Virgil was desperate and finally dove underneath the coffee table. He pulled the strings as tight as he could on his hoodie until only his eyes were showing.

"You don't have to speak now, Virgil; whenever you're ready, there's no pressure," Nurse Lovington said.

"I wanted to announce that I'm starting a new company online. I'm going to sell placebos to the world," Drake said.

"While you're online, see if you can goggle something about pot-bellied pigs," Potbelly said.

"Will do," Drake said.

"Okay, would anyone else like to speak?" Nurse Lovington asked.

Godot stood up to speak; but his lips fell off before he could, so he just sat back down.

"I'll sew those back on for you later, Godot," Nurse Lovington said.

Godot shook his head in acquiescence.

"I would like to say that I am supposed to be released on the next leap day, so it would be nice if we could have a farewell party," Crazy Bob said.

Everyone clapped at this. They loved Crazy Bob's farewell parties; and since he'd been there, he had had eighty-two of them. The bulletin board had pictures from all of them. In the 80s pictures he had teased hair, in the 90s it was oily during the grunge phase and in the 00s he had practically no hair.

"That sounds great, Robert; I'll bring the cupcakes," Nurse Lovington said.

"Can you bring soda too?" Abram asked.

"Of course, Abram, I'll bring in two liter sodas; and you can have one all to yourself," Nurse Lovington said.

"I'll bring in donuts," Lester said.

Everyone knew that Lester, who chronically lied, wasn't going to bring anything. He always said he was going to bring something and never did.

"Okay, unless anyone has anything to add, I think we are finished with circle time today," Nurse Lovington said.

Everyone dispersed from the dayroom except for Virgil, who was still lying flat on his stomach under the coffee table peeping out of his hoodie.

Chapter 28

Nurse Lovington was going to Dr. Olive's office to ask him about getting a pot-bellied pig for Richard. She was a little angry at Dr. Olive for telling him he could have one and then turning right around and taking it back. It was a cruel thing to do. She barged right in without even knocking.

The real Dr. Olive was not in his office, but Dr. Mannequin Olive was sitting at his desk. His hairpiece was still on backwards from when Drake had knocked it off. It gave him a 1960s Beatles look.

"Dr. Olive, I think it was a really rotten thing you did, telling Richard he could have a pot-bellied pig one minute and then turning right around and rescinding the whole thing. Don't you know that is the only thing the poor man lives for?" Nurse Lovington said.

Dr. Mannequin Olive just stared at her cheekily underneath his mop top.

Nurse Lovington was flustered. She was angry, but she also found this new attitude of Dr. Olive's attractive. His demeanor was cool, and his direct gaze made him seem suave.

She strode up to his desk and slapped him, and then the next thing she did surprised herself even more.

Nurse Lovington sat down on Dr. Mannequin Olive's lap and kissed him passionately.

"Oh, my god. Dr. Olive. I am so sorry; I don't know what came over me. I swear I won't let it happen again. Please don't write me up," Nurse Lovington said.

Nurse Lovington stared at him with tears in her eyes, so overwrought with her emotions that it didn't dawn on her that this wasn't the real Dr. Olive; it was the mannequin that she had taken out of the closet just the other day.

Dr. Mannequin Olive, who was unfazed by the whole thing, stared back with his suave, handsome face. It was too much for Nurse Lovington, and she kissed him again.

She ran out of Dr. Olive/Mannequin Olive's office ashamed and confused. Potbelly touched her on the shoulder, startling her.

"Nurse Lovington, are you okay? You look white as a sheet!" Potbelly asked.

"Yes, I'm okay, Richard. I think I just need to go home for today and lie down."

"Did you ask Dr. Olive about my getting a pot-bellied pig?" Potbelly asked.

"I did, Richard," Nurse Lovington said.

"Well, what did he say?" Potbelly asked.

"He didn't say 'yes' or 'no'; I think he has a lot on his plate right now. I'll talk to him again later when I'm in a better frame of mind," Nurse Lovington said.

"Okay, I guess that's better than 'no,'" Potbelly said.

Potbelly watched Nurse Lovington leave, and he decided he was going to go into Dr. Olive's office and demand an answer once and for all.

"I know you're busy, Dr. Olive, but a simple 'yes' or 'no' on the subject will do," Potbelly said.

No response from the shaggy-haired Dr. Olive, who now, thanks to Nurse Lovington, had red lipstick smeared all over his lips. Potbelly was not deterred; he was going to stand there until he received an answer.

He stared into the black holes of Dr. Mannequin Olive to search for his answer. He thought that Dr. Olive winked at him, but it may have just been him who blinked.

"Hey, what's going on?" Drake said.

Drake had walked in on the staring contest between Potbelly and Dr. Mannequin Olive.

"I'm waiting for Dr. Olive to answer my question about whether or not I can have a pot-bellied pig," Potbelly said.

"Dr. Olive, are you wearing lipstick?" Drake asked.

"What difference does it make if he's wearing lipstick or not?" Potbelly asked.

"I just wondered because it looks like the same kind Nurse Lovington wears," Drake said.

"Oh, my god. He forced himself on Nurse Lovington," Potbelly said.

"I wouldn't jump to conclusions," Drake said.

"I just bumped into Nurse Lovington as she was leaving. She was pale as a ghost, and she had been crying," Potbelly said.

"You scoundrel, you forced yourself on poor Nurse Lovington," Drake said.

Potbelly leaned over Dr. Mannequin Olive's desk and grabbed him by the shoulders and shook him until his wig fell off. Drake punched him in the side of the face and knocked him out of his chair and onto the floor.

"Confess, you snake!" Potbelly yelled.

"What the hell is going on in here?" Dr. Boyd yelled.

Dr. Boyd, who had heard yelling, ran down the hall from his office to see what all the commotion was about. He looked at disheveled Dr. Mannequin Olive, who was bald and wearing red lipstick, lying on the floor, to Drake and Potbelly, who looked deranged.

He quickly made an assessment; and without warning, Dr. Boyd plunged a syringe into Drake's arm and one into Potbelly's butt as he was still leaning over Dr. Olive's desk. Drake, Potbelly and Dr. Mannequin Olive were all passed out on the floor.

This place is an insane asylum, Dr. Boyd thought.

He turned out the light in Dr. Olive's office and closed the door.

Dr. Olive had just come back from seeing Lester, even though he was Dr. Boyd's patient, as part of his new double secret therapy. He walked into his office and flipped on the light and surveyed the scene.

"What the hell is going on?" Dr. Olive asked.

Potbelly was just coming to, and then Drake started to moan.

Potbelly looked up at Dr. Olive and then at Dr. Mannequin Olive on the floor.

"What happened?" Potbelly asked.

"I asked you the same question," Dr. Olive said.

"Wake up, Drake!" Potbelly screamed.

Drake, startled by Potbelly's yelling, was now alert.

"Look, Drake, there are two Dr. Olives," Potbelly said.

Drake looked at the Dr. Olive standing in the doorway and the Dr. Olive lying down on the floor with no hair.

"Dr. Olive, I didn't know you had a twin," Drake said.

"I don't; that is a mannequin," Dr. Olive said.

"Why is there a mannequin in your office?" Drake asked.

"He is me when I'm not in the office," Dr. Olive said.

"But how can a mannequin be you?" Potbelly asked.

"I have been very busy, and Dr. Mannequin Olive has been helping me with my caseload," Dr. Olive said.

"I've been having therapy with a mannequin?" Potbelly asked.

"Like I said; he is me when I'm not here," Dr. Olive said.

"But he's not a doctor," Potbelly said.

"He has a degree from John Hopkins University. Honestly, Richard, do you think I would leave my patients with an unqualified mannequin?" Dr. Olive said.

"I want to see a copy of his degree," Drake said.

Dr. Olive walked over to the framed diploma on his wall and took it down.

"Here is his diploma," Dr. Olive said.

"That's your diploma," Drake said.

"Precisely. He is me; therefore, we have the same credentials," Dr. Olive said.

To erase any further doubt, he picked up Dr. Mannequin Olive and put him back in his chair; and then he put his wig back on and pointed to the name *Dr. Olive* stitched on the lab coat.

"I guess the lab coat doesn't lie," Potbelly said.

"You still didn't answer my question about what is going on in here," Dr. Olive said.

"When I got here, Nurse Lovington was upset and she had been crying. I came in here to ask once and for all if I could have a pot-bellied pig. Then Drake showed up and realized that Dr. Olive—I mean Dr. Mannequin Olive—was wearing Nurse Lovington's lipstick, so we came to the conclusion that he forced himself on her. Why else would she be so upset?" Potbelly said.

"We were going to beat a confession out of him—I mean you—but then Dr. Boyd came in and gave us a sedative," Drake said.

"What makes you think that he came on to Nurse Lovington? I mean he is me when I'm not in the office, and do you think I would do something like that?" Dr. Olive said.

"Are you saying Nurse Lovington came on to you?" Potbelly asked.

"I don't know; we seem to be making a lot of assumptions here," Dr. Olive said.

"Yes, and you know what happens when you assume things," Drake said.

"Crazy Bob told me what happens; he said, 'You make a pair of asses out of you and me,'" Potbelly said.

"How can we make a pair of asses when there are three of us?" Drake asked.

"It's a metaphor," Dr. Olive said.

"Now I get it," Drake said.

"So can I?" Potbelly asked.

"Can you what?" Dr. Olive asked.

"Can I have a pot-bellied pig?" Potbelly asked.

Dr. Olive sighed. He was tired of fighting this battle with Richard.

"No, Richard, I'm afraid it isn't a good idea. This is my final answer on the subject," Dr. Olive said.

Drake walked Potbelly back to his room. Drake tried to pat him on the back and say reassuring words, but it was hopeless; Potbelly was inconsolable.

"You'll get another pot-bellied pig someday," Drake said.

"No, I won't. I work for Looney Bin Incorporated, so I won't ever get one. I won't get married or have kids; I won't even get paid," Potbelly said.

"Do you know what the clown from the Big Apple Circus used to sing when I was upset?" Drake asked.

"You mean the clown that tried to molest you?" Potbelly asked.

"No, this was Bessy the Clown; she had one leg a little shorter than the other and walked with a limp," Drake said.

"What did Bessy sing to you?" Potbelly asked.

"She sang, 'Always look on the bright side of life,'" Drake said.

"The Monty Python song?" Potbelly asked.

"I can't remember all the words, but I'll whistle it for you."

Potbelly nodded his head so Drake began to whistle.

Drake had good lungs and could whistle loudly. Crazy Bob, who was in his room, heard the whistling and started to whistle also.

Potbelly smiled despite himself and whistled along. The only lines that Drake remembered were, "Life's a piece of shit, when you look at it. Always look on the bright side of life."

This was the line that always made him giggle every time Bessy the Clown sang it.

When they were done whistling, Drake put his arm on Potbelly's shoulder.

"It will be okay; we are going to get you a pot-bellied pig one way or another," Drake said.

Chapter 29

Virgil, formerly Virgil from solitary confinement, had been unconfined for two weeks now. He was in the dayroom and was going to hide under one of the tables, but he noticed Drake sitting at a table with Crazy Bob and Potbelly. They were painting something on the eggs. His curiosity was greater than his fear, and he approached their table.

"What are you doing?" Virgil whispered.

"I'm painting faces on eggs; it's a passion of mine. Why are you whispering?" Drake asked.

"I don't want them to hear me," Virgil said.

"You don't want who to hear you?" Potbelly asked.

"I don't want the voices in my head to hear me," Virgil said.

"Okay, I'll whisper too. I don't want the voices inside your head to hear me either," Potbelly said.

"We will all whisper," Crazy Bob said.

"Sit down and join us," Potbelly whispered.

"I prefer to get underneath the table," Virgil whispered.

"Suit yourself," Drake whispered.

"Why were you in solitary confinement?" Crazy Bob asked in a whisper.

"I like it," Virgil whispered.

"You were in there by choice?" Crazy Bob asked, still whispering.

"Yes, I prefer to be in solitary confinement. Dr. Boyd lets me stay in there but insists that I come out sometimes to socialize because it's good for my well-being," Virgil whispered.

"So, are you a recluse?" Drake asked in a whisper.

"Well, you can't really be a recluse when you have people talking inside your head all the time," Virgil whispered.

"That's very true," Potbelly said.

"I'm glad you're out because we have been meaning to ask you about your writing. We need to see it so we can compare it to the other legendary Virgil and see who has the better work," Crazy Bob said.

"What writing?" Virgil asked.

"Don't you write?" Drake asked.

"No, I don't," Virgil whispered.

"But your name is Virgil. How can you have that great name if you don't write?" Crazy Bob asked.

"Well, your name is Bob. How come you don't sing like Bob Dylan? Lots of people have the same names as someone famous but don't necessary do what they do for a living," Virgil whispered.

"I see your point. What did you do for a living?" Crazy Bob asked.

"I made wax figures for museums," Virgil whispered.

Drake gave a soft whistle.

"Wow, what a great profession. What figures did you make?" Drake asked.

"I made mostly famous or historical people," Virgil whispered.

"Could you make a Virgil out of wax?" Potbelly asked.

"Sure, if I had a picture of him, wax and some clay. I couldn't do a full-size one here, though, because of the logistics of it; but I could do a basic head model," Virgil whispered.

"Can you also make a pot-bellied pig?" Potbelly asked.

"I only do people," Virgil whispered.

"Nurse Lovington can get you everything you need," Drake whispered.

"Except books on pot-bellied pigs," Potbelly whispered.

"What are you going to do with just a head?" Virgil asked.

"He could dictate to me since I'm the one who taught at Dartmouth. I will write it out in shorthand, and Godot will type it up for us," Crazy Bob.

"Godot can't read shorthand," Drake whispered.

"Exactly, it's the perfect system," Crazy Bob whispered.

"How is a wax figure going to talk?" Drake asked.

"The wax figures in my head talk to me constantly," Virgil whispered.

"You have wax in your head?" Potbelly asked.

"Yes, all good wax makers have wax in their heads," Virgil whispered.

"I have wax in my ears," Potbelly whispered.

"You can't really make anything with that kind of wax. That's just your ears sweating," Virgil whispered.

"My ears sweat?" Potbelly asked.

"I have a placebo for that," Drake whispered.

"I'll take two since I have two ears," Potbelly whispered.

Potbelly handed over $40, and Drake put it in the fanny pack he was wearing.

"I like your fanny pack," Potbelly whispered.

"Thanks, I asked Nurse Lovington to give me one so I can keep my placebos and cash in it," Drake whispered.

"Why is everyone whispering?" Lester asked in a whisper.

No one had seen Lester; he had snuck up to their table.

"Oh, Lester, I didn't see you there. Lester, this is Virgil," Crazy Bob pointed underneath the table.

"Virgil, this is Lester. He is a lying Sagittarius," Crazy Bob said.

"We don't want the voices in Virgil's head to hear what we are saying," Drake said.

"I hear voices sometimes," Lester whispered.

"When do you hear voices?" Drake asked.

"I hear voices right now," Lester whispered.

"Those are our voices. Virgil hears wax figure voices," Crazy Bob whispered.

"Oh, I don't hear any of those," Lester whispered.

"Virgil is going to make a wax figure head of the writer Virgil," Crazy Bob whispered.

"Why him?" Lester asked.

"We figure he still has some great writing left in him. Besides, he could give us all a tour of hell," Crazy Bob whispered.

"I didn't know we gave tours," Lester whispered.

"Not this hell. I mean the other hell, the biblical one," Crazy Bob whispered.

"I don't have any sunblock," Potbelly whispered.

"Don't worry about it; it's a dry heat," Crazy Bob whispered.

"Do you think my Virgil will be as great a writer and orator as the original?" Virgil asked.

"Well, there are two Dr. Olives; and I think the new one is even better than the old one," Drake said.

"I think the old one is bipolar," Potbelly said.

"There are two Dr. Olives?" Crazy Bob asked in excitement.

He forgot to whisper, and Virgil put his hand over his ears.

"There are two Dr. Olives?" Crazy Bob whispered it this time.

"There are Dr. Olive and Dr. Mannequin Olive, except technically there are not two of him since Dr. Olive says that when he is not in his office, Dr. Mannequin Olive is him; therefore, they are the same person," Potbelly said.

"They are identical in appearance but vastly different in their personalities," Drake said.

"I prefer Dr. Mannequin Olive; he's more attentive and patient," Potbelly said.

"I prefer Dr. Mannequin Olive as well," Drake said.

"So he is like a Dr. Jekyll and Mr. Hyde?" Crazy Bob asked.

"Is Dr. Jekyll the doctor that removed Abram's appendix?" Drake asked.

"You're thinking of Dr. Jackal. No, he's like himself but he's not himself," Drake said.

"That is the exact story of Dr. Jekyll and Mr. Hyde. It was the same doctor; only one was good and the other was bad," Crazy Bob said.

"How bad?" Drake asked.

"He killed people," Crazy Bob said.

"Dr. Olive kills people?" Drake asked.

"If one of them is like Dr. Hyde," Crazy Bob said.

"I think Dr. Olive is more like Dr. Hyde," Drake said.

"Me too; I think there is a darkness that lurks in his heart," Potbelly said.

"You're lucky you don't have him as a doctor, Crazy Bob," Drake said.

"I wasn't supposed to say anything; but in light of recent revelations, I am seeing Dr. Olive as well. He says it's part of his new double secret therapy program," Crazy Bob said.

"I'm seeing Dr. Olive as well, and he told me the same thing," Lester said.

"We have to report Dr. Olive to the board of Looney Bin Incorporated," Drake said.

"I think he is dangerous; he forced himself on Nurse Lovington," Potbelly said.

"It was Dr. Mannequin Olive who was wearing Nurse Lovington's lipstick," Drake reminded him.

"Why was he wearing lipstick?" Lester asked.

"Maybe he's a cross-dresser," Potbelly suggested.

"Maybe she threw herself at him," Drake said.

"Yes, but the most logical answer is that if Dr. Olive is like Dr. Hyde, he put Nurse Lovington's lipstick on Dr. Mannequin Olive to frame him," Crazy Bob said.

"Okay, it's settled; we have to inform the board that Dr. Olive is really Dr. Hyde and is attempting to murder someone and frame Dr. Mannequin Olive as a cross-dresser," Potbelly said.

Potbelly had come to the logical conclusion, and they all agreed.

Chapter 30

It was time for Crazy Bob's farewell party. He was leaving the day before the next full moon. Nurse Lovington brought in the food, drinks and party games. There was a piñata hanging up, and each of the patients was taking a whack at it. It was Lester's turn. He slowly crept up on the piñata as if it might hear him and decide to run away. If ever a piñata were going to run away, it would be from this group of lunatics. Lester missed the piñata but whacked Crazy Bob in the head.

"Ouch!" Crazy Bob yelled.

"Did I get it?" Lester asked, removing his blindfold.

"No, you hit me," Crazy Bob said.

"Do you have any candy inside your head?" Lester asked.

"No candy, just fart bugs," Crazy Bob said.

"What do they taste like?" Lester said.

"A little sour," Crazy Bob said.

Lester passed the blindfold and the stick to Fritz.

"Nein. I don't like ze blindfold. It remindz me of a firing zquad," Fritz said.

He gave the blindfold and stick to Godot. Godot was only wearing his top hat, but other than that he was completely naked. He told Nurse Lovington that he lost his underwear, along with his pants and vest. He suspected that someone was stealing his clothes; but considering he was a good five inches taller than the tallest person there, it was unlikely.

Godot tried to put the blindfold on; but his fingers kept falling off, so he offered the blindfold and stick to Sam.

Sam put the blindfold on and spun around a few times so he would be disoriented and not be able to make an immediate beeline for the piñata.

"I will hit it with the stick. I will get it with one lick," Sam said.

He walked over to where he thought it was and swung. He did succeed in hitting it with one lick as he predicted. He tore the piñata in half with one mighty blow.

"And David struck the Philistine and killed him," Drake said.

"Who's the Philistine?" Crazy Bob asked.

"That's what they call people from Philadelphia," Potbelly said.

Crazy Bob examined the piñata.

"It says it was made in China," Crazy Bob said.

Nurse Lovington forgot to buy the candy so instead of candy, it was stuffed full of gauze. Gauze rained down everywhere like a snow storm. A piece fell near Virgil who was underneath the table. He picked it up and put it in his mouth.

Crazy Bob turned on the CD player and ABBA's song "Dancing Queen" filled the room. Nurse Lovington hung up a disco ball; and everyone danced except Virgil, who remained underneath the table, and Abram, who was busy consuming all the free soda.

Crazy Bob grabbed Nurse Lovington and spun her around the floor in the dayroom. Drake and Potbelly were imitating John Travolta's moves from *Saturday Night Fever*. Sam was doing the YMCA dance, which was the only dance he knew and did to every song. Godot started to dance; but his leg kept falling off, so he just sat naked in a chair and tapped his remaining toes.

Lester was doing a dance that resembled the mashed potato. Fritz, who had on lederhosen for the occasion, was doing some sort of traditional Bavarian dance where he lifted his leg and slapped the bottom of his shoe.

Nurse Lovington sat down to catch her breath and snap some photos with her phone, so Crazy Bob danced solo. He had no ear for music or rhythm, for that matter; all his steps were out of time, and he missed the beat when he tried to clap.

They danced for over an hour. Just when the party was beginning to fizzle, a beautiful young blond walked in wearing a white uniform like Nurse Lovington; but instead of squeaky shoes, she was wearing white pumps. Also, unlike Nurse Lovington, she had her dress unzipped really far down in the front to reveal a more than ample bosom. She was obviously not your typical nurse, but she was carrying a medical bag.

"Who is Crazy Bob?" Stripper Nurse asked.

Everyone shouted at the same time except Nurse Lovington, who was trying to silence them.

"I'm sorry, Ms., but this is a place of business. We don't allow that kind of thing in here. You must have the wrong place," Nurse Lovington said.

"Is this Looney Bin Incorporated?" Stripper Nurse asked.

"Yes, it is," Nurse Lovington said.

"Then this is the place," Stripper Nurse said.

"Who called you?" Nurse Lovington asked.

"A Dr. P.R. Noid called me and told me that I was to come in

115

today for a going-away party for Crazy Bob," Stripper Nurse said.

"We don't have a Dr. P.R. Noid on staff," Nurse Lovington said.

"Oh, come on, Nurse Lovington. It's Crazy Bob's going-away party. Let the man enjoy a little harmless fun," Drake said.

It was Drake and Potbelly's idea to get the stripper for Crazy Bob. They wanted to do something different for this party, something to really liven it up.

"Please," shouted everyone.

"Okay, but I want it on record that I disapprove of this," Nurse Lovington said.

Crazy Bob wrote down in his notebook of conversations that Nurse Lovington was a party pooper.

"Who is our special boy?" Stripper Nurse asked.

"He's right there," Potbelly said.

Potbelly pointed to Crazy Bob, who was sitting in a chair. His bald head was glistening with sweat; and he was wearing a flannel green shirt, jeans and a grin. Stripper Nurse went to dim the lights. The disco ball and Crazy Bob's head were the only two lights shining in the room. Stripper Nurse played some music of her own. It was some kind of generic house music that they played at clubs, with its endless thump, thump, thump.

Stripper Nurse started to gyrate in front of Crazy Bob. She removed a stethoscope from her medical bag and wrapped it around Crazy Bob's neck as she pushed his head down almost in her cleavage.

Everyone was clapping and cheering for Crazy Bob except for Nurse Lovington, who was wearing a disapproving frown. Even Virgil had come out from underneath the table to watch the show.

Lester reached in his pocket and pulled out a rolled-up joint, which he had saved for such an occasion. He sparked up, took a toke and passed it around.

Stripper Nurse plunged a thermometer into Crazy Bob's mouth and then unbuckled his pants. She slid them down to reveal a pair of Mickey Mouse boxers. She leaned him over the chair and began to spank him.

With all the hooting and hollering, no one saw Dr. Raven, chairman of the board of Looney Bin Inc., walk in. He was wearing a tailor-made suit that looked very expensive.

He walked right up to the Stripper Nurse who was still whacking Crazy Bob on his butt like the piñata from earlier.

Before Dr. Raven could speak, she stopped spanking Crazy Bob and turned her sights on him. She began to unbutton Dr. Raven's shirt and started grinding on his leg.

"What is going on here?" Dr. Raven demanded.

Nurse Lovington leaped up to turn off the music.

Stripper Nurse, who wasn't the least bit perturbed at having her act interrupted, continued to gyrate. He started to say something else, but Stripper Nurse removed a band-aid from her bag and placed it on his lips. He ripped off the band-aid.

"What is going on here?" he shouted again.

Crazy Bob pulled up his pants, and Nurse Lovington was in tears.

"I'm so sorry, Dr. Raven; I told them I disapproved of all of this," Nurse Lovington said.

"Who are you?" Potbelly asked.

"I'm Dr. Raven. I'm a board member of Looney Bin Incorporated, and I've come to follow up on several anonymous complaints against Dr. Olive and launch an investigation," Dr. Raven said.

"Oh yeah, I remember you from the commercial day," Potbelly said.

"I'm so sorry, Dr. Raven; I had no idea that you were coming," Nurse Lovington said.

"Obviously. Now I want this young lady to leave, and I would like some answers to my questions starting with…is that young man smoking pot?"

Dr. Raven pointed to Lester, who was still puffing away.

"Lester! Put that out this instant!" Nurse Lovington yelled.

The stripper nurse put all her equipment back in her bag and strutted out the door. All eyes were on the buxom blonde nurse, whose legs went on forever and whose curves should have been illegal.

"Now, would someone explain to me what's going on around here? I mean, is this a mental rehabilitation facility or a fraternity?" Dr. Raven asked.

"What's a mental rehabilitation facility?" Crazy Bob asked.

"He means insane asylum," Drake said.

"Oh. Well, we are all perfectly sane and of sound mind here," Crazy Bob said.

"We were having a farewell party for Richard here, and things

117

got a little out of hand," Nurse Lovington said.

"A little out of hand? Nurse Lovington, you'll be lucky if I don't have your nursing license revoked. Why is that man naked and wearing a top hat?" Dr. Raven asked.

"Someone stole my clothes," Godot said.

"Please, Dr. Raven, don't blame Nurse Lovington; she didn't know about the stripper, and she thoroughly disapproved. She's a good nurse; in fact, she is the best nurse who has ever been in this place," Drake said.

"She may have disapproved, but she did nothing. Where are Dr. Olive and Dr. Boyd?" Dr. Raven asked.

"You forgot Dr. Mannequin Olive," Potbelly said.

"Who is Dr. Mannequin Olive?" Dr. Raven asked.

"He is Dr. Olive when Dr. Olive is too busy to see his regular patients because he is seeing Dr. Boyd's patients for double secret therapy," Crazy Bob said.

"What are you people talking about? This is the nuttiest nut house I've ever seen. I'm going to find Dr. Olive and get to the bottom of this mannequin business," Dr Raven said.

Dr. Raven stormed out of the room. Nurse Lovington began to cry, and Potbelly patted her on the shoulder.

"There, there, Nurse Lovington, don't you worry about a thing. We will fix this; you're not going anywhere," Potbelly said.

Lester went over to pour Nurse Lovington a drink, but all the soda bottles were empty. Lester was about to ask what happened to all the soda when Abram let out an ear-shattering belch.

Lester reached into his pocket and pulled out a small bottle of vodka, which he saved for occasions just as this. He poured a little in a plastic cup and handed it to her.

"Thank you, Lester. I don't know, boys; it looks like my goose is cooked this time," Nurse Lovington said.

"I could go for some goose," Abram said as he belched.

Chapter 31

Dr. Olive was sitting at his desk going over some of his notes while Dr. Mannequin Olive was sitting beside him in a chair, not going over notes or doing anything at all but looking straight ahead. No one could go over notes like Dr. Olive; he was very thorough. And no one could stare straight ahead like Dr. Mannequin Olive; he was equally as thorough.

Dr. Raven knocked on the door. He had a specific purpose for being here today and it wasn't to cook Nurse Lovington's goose; he had bigger goose to fry.

"Come in," Dr. Olive said.

Dr. Raven walked in. He had blonde hair with a little gray around the temples and bright blue eyes. He is what Fritz would refer to as the perfect Aryan specimen.

"Dr. Raven. I didn't know you were coming. Are you here about the report I submitted, specifically about how many extra clients I've been seeing? The results have been amazing. The patients are getting double the therapy and getting better at twice the rate," Dr. Olive said.

"I would like to discuss that, but I'm also following up on another matter," Dr. Raven said.

"Allow me to introduce my alter ego, if you will, Dr. Mannequin Olive," Dr. Olive said.

Dr. Raven shook hands with Dr. Mannequin Olive. "You have a firm grip," Dr. Raven said approvingly.

"I wondered if you both had time for some questions," Dr. Raven said.

"Of course," Dr. Olive said.

"I have the figures that you submitted to the board last week," Dr. Raven said.

He took them out of his briefcase.

"The overall wellness rate has increased by 42% in just the short amount of time you've instituted your new policy of double secret therapy," Dr. Raven said.

"Yes, I've noticed a dramatic improvement in all the patients," Dr. Olive said.

"The board members and I wonder why you wanted it kept secret from Dr. Boyd since it was his patients you were seeing, as well as your own?" Dr. Raven asked.

"Well, I just wanted it secret until I had your approval, and then I was going to let him know. It was just a testing period to see how the double therapy would work out, and I think you will agree with me that it is a marketable success.

"You wanted to wait until you had our approval, but yet you went ahead with it without the board's consent?" Dr. Raven asked.

"Perhaps I was just a little overzealous, but I only had the patients' welfare in mine. Again, you can't argue with the results," Dr. Olive said.

"Actually, I can argue with the results. Do you know what it is that we do here, Dr. Olive?" Dr. Raven asked.

"Yes, of course. We treat the mentally ill," Dr. Olive said.

"Yes, but what is our goal?" Dr. Raven asked.

"I'm afraid I don't understand you," Dr. Olive said.

"Well, it says it right there in our letterhead," Dr. Raven said.

Dr. Raven pointed to the letterhead on Dr. Olive's desk.

"Making crazy a mission," Dr. Olive read.

"That's right; crazy is our mission. How can we make crazy our mission if your mission is to make them all better? We are working at cross-purposes," Dr. Raven said.

"So you're saying you don't want the patients to be cured?" Dr. Olive said.

"I want the patients to be treated. You've got overall wellness up 42%; therefore sickness is down 42%, and that's not good. The value of our stock has declined since you've instituted your little program, and the shares have been selling at below par," Dr. Raven said.

"Well, I assure you, Dr. Raven and the other board members, that I will cease my program at once," Dr. Olive said.

"The other reason why I'm here is that I've been receiving alarming reports," Dr. Raven said.

"What reports?" Dr. Olive asked.

"They range from sexual assault to murder," Dr. Raven said.

"That's just ludicrous; I've never sexually assaulted anyone, and I've certainly never murdered anyone," Dr. Olive said.

Dr. Mannequin Olive just stared ahead, remaining prudently quiet all this time.

"Patients have reported strange behavior coming from this office. They say you've been telling them one thing and then recanting it the next. They say that you are patient and nurturing to them one minute, and flippant and exasperated with them the next. Your behavior has been described as increasingly extreme and erratic, demonstrating bipolar behavior," Dr. Raven said.

Dr. Olive was on his feet. "I've done no such thing. It simply isn't true," Dr. Olive said.

Dr. Raven smiled.

"We want the patients here at Looney Bin Incorporated to be crazy and have a satisfactory well-being, enough to distract them from the fact that they are not getting paid because why should they work for us for free, when they can work anywhere else for money? If they are well, then they don't really need us. There is a fine balance to be maintained. It's all about nuance."

"Nuance, sir?" Dr. Olive asked.

"Yes, nuance. I believe that Dr. Mannequin Olive here knows exactly what I mean," Dr. Raven said.

"He doesn't know anything, sir; he's a mannequin," Dr. Olive said.

"On the contrary; I think he knows all about nuance. Dr. Olive, I'd like to have a word alone with Dr. Mannequin Olive," Dr. Raven said.

Dr. Olive looked incredulously at Dr. Raven and then at Dr. Mannequin Olive.

"Why do you want to speak to Dr. Mannequin Olive?" Dr. Olive asked.

"That is between Dr. Mannequin Olive and me," Dr. Raven said.

Dr. Olive couldn't believe what was happening here. Why did Dr. Raven want to speak with this mannequin? He rose with all the dignity he could muster and left his own office. Dr. Raven looked coyly at Dr. Mannequin Olive, who had remained as cool as a cucumber.

"God, that man is a buffoon. I never wanted to hire him; my every instinct told me not to, but we were short-staffed at the time. You seem like a smart fellow," Dr. Raven said.

Dr. Mannequin Olive just remained seated, looking like a smart fellow.

"Yes, I can see you know which way the wind is blowing. I came here with a problem, and now I think I've found a solution. Dr. Olive's patients have been complaining about strange behavior. A Dr. Jekyll and Mr. Hyde, if you will. We don't need both of them; and I think Dr. Olive is our Mr. Hyde, and we need a Dr. Jekyll. I want you to be our Dr. Jekyll. I am going to fire Dr. Olive, and I've come here to do precisely that and more. I believe Dr. Olive has become unhinged as a result of stress, and I am removing him from his staff position and admitting him as a patient. I want you to take his position, along with a five percent raise. The reports have been all bad about Mr. Hyde, but the reports about Dr. Jekyll have been glowing. Many patients have reported that their sessions, that I assume were with you, as having been the best and most productive they've ever had. Although we don't want them cured, we do want them treated and kept happy. What do you say? I can have a contract drawn up," Dr. Raven said.

Dr. Mannequin Olive remained silent and made no movements.

"I see you're an old-fashioned man. I'm an old-fashioned man myself," Dr. Raven said.

"What do you say we shake on it like real men?"

Dr. Raven shook Dr. Mannequin Olive's hand.

"You do have a firm grip. A firm grip indeed. Yes, I think you are going to do quite well," Dr. Raven said.

Chapter 32

Virgil from solitary confinement, whose last name was coincidentally Solitary Confinement, had an appointment with Dr. Mannequin Olive.

Virgil walked in, and immediately got under Dr. Mannequin Olive's desk. Dr. Mannequin Olive was a laid-back kind of guy and didn't seem to mind. He didn't mind if you were late to appointments or missed them all together. In fact, he didn't mind much of anything. Virgil stayed underneath Dr. Mannequin Olive's desk for the first ten minutes of his session before he got the courage to peek out. Dr. Mannequin Olive knew the right approach to take with Virgil. It was best to let him speak first; otherwise, he might get too overwhelmed and clam up in his shell.

"I used to work in a wax museum. I designed and made all the figures," Virgil said.

He looked up at Dr. Mannequin Olive, who was listening attentively, so he continued, "I once made a figure of my wife. We're divorced now. After the divorce, I threw the wax figure of my wife over a bridge into a lake. Someone thought I was throwing a real person in the lake and dove in after her. The man who dove in after her hit his head on a rock and fell into a coma. That was five years ago, and the last I heard he was still in a coma," Virgil said.

He searched Dr. Mannequin Olive's face for any signs of disapproval.

"I know what you're thinking; but no, I'm not a Pisces. I'm actually an Aries," Virgil said.

This wasn't at all what Dr. Mannequin Olive was thinking.

"I also made wax fruit for a number of years and sold it to department stores. I'm not sure why it was so popular to have wax fruit on your coffee table or dining table. I never liked the taste of wax fruit; I always thought real fruit tasted better, but to each his own."

He looked at Dr. Mannequin Olive, who appeared to be winking at him; but it was probably because he was squinting. He was nearsighted and needed glasses.

"I have to say you are probably the most laid-back and hippest doctor I've ever had. My old doctor used to tell me I was crazier than a bed bug and was hopeless. Come to think of it, I've never had a doctor; that was my parents who used to say that.

"You probably think my parents named me after the great poet Virgil; but actually I was named after a trucker whom my mom met in a bar and had an affair with, who may or may not be my father. The bar was called Sloppy Joes, and it was a trucker's bar. She almost named me Sloppy Joe but thought better of it. She thought I might get teased with a name like that.

"I was teased, though, not because of my name but because of what all of my teachers described as my *peculiarities*. I never liked playing outside with the other kids. I just liked making things out of Play-Doh.

"One time I made the face of a girl I didn't like, and I showed it to her. Her name was Margaret; and she liked it and thought it was really nice, until I put the Play-Doh face on the floor, pulled my pants down and urinated on it. She began to cry, and I got suspended from school for three days for that. I was sent to the principal's office, and they called my father.

"My father drank a lot, and he was drunk when they called him in. My father was outraged at the principal and my teacher. He called them communists and said how dare they censor his son's artistic freedom and didn't they know a genius when they saw one. It was the first and only time my father stood up for me.

"I later regretted urinating on Margaret's Play-Doh face because it turned out she had a crush on me. So from that day forth, I never urinated again on any of the faces I created. All the wax figures I created over the years, I kept in a pristine and urine-free condition. Except for my wife's; I threw hers into a lake, as I said. I never saw Margaret again after that; my father took me out of that school. I wish I knew where she was now and how she was doing. I would love to make her a new wax face and present it to her as a gift and apologize for pissing on the old one."

Virgil sighed, and a single tear fell from the corner of his eye.

"I won't take up any more of your time; I know you are a busy man."

Dr. Mannequin Olive was a very busy man, and indeed Virgil had taken up a fifteen-minute chunk of it.

Virgil crawled out from underneath Dr. Mannequin Olive's desk and stood at the door.

"I noticed you don't have any wax fruit on your desk. I'll make some for you and bring it the next time I see you."

Chapter 33

"Just take your time; no need to rush into anything," Dr. Boyd said.

Dr. Boyd smiled. He relished every moment of the former doctor's anguish. Dr. Olive was no longer Dr. Olive but just simply Frank Olive, the patient.

"I have nothing to say to you. You're a quack, and your methods are unorthodox," Frank said.

"You say I'm the quack, but here I sit in my own office with my name 'Dr. Boyd' stitched on my coat; and here you sit on the other side of my desk," Dr. Boyd said.

"I was helping patients get better. Your patients were improving rapidly under my care. It's not my fault this organization is crooked and doesn't want its patients to improve," Frank said.

"It's not the organization's fault. Your own patients turned against you. They much prefer Dr. Mannequin Olive, and so do I; he's a swell fellow," Dr. Boyd said.

"How can that be? He is me and I am him. What he knows, I know. How can you like one and not the other?" Dr. Olive asked.

"It is just like Dr. Jekyll and Mr. Hyde. You have split personalities and who knows? If your Mr. Hyde had continued on in the direction you were headed, you might have murdered someone," Dr. Boyd said.

"Don't be ridiculous. I would never murder anyone, but at this moment I wouldn't mind murdering you," Frank said.

"Oh, is that so? Dr. Boyd opened his desk drawer and removed his tape recorder. I think when the board hears this, they will definitely agree with my assessment that you are a danger to others and need to be removed from the general population and put into isolation," Dr. Boyd said.

"No, you can't do that. I won't go," Frank said.

Dr. Boyd picked up his phone and buzzed Nurse Lovington.

"Nurse Lovington, could you please have security escort patient Frank Olive to isolation. Thank you," Dr. Boyd said.

"There is nothing wrong with me," Frank said.

Two security guards walked in and placed their hands on Frank's shoulders.

"No, I won't go," Frank said.

He began to struggle and wriggle his shoulders away from the guards.

"I'm afraid you have no choice; you are too violent to remain with the other patients," Dr. Boyd said.

Dr. Boyd reached into his lab coat for one of his syringes that were usually reserved for Abram. The guards held him down in his seat while Dr. Boyd plunged the needle in his arm. It only took a moment for the sedative to work its way into his blood stream. He stopped struggling and melted like butter into the arms of the security guards. They picked up Frank, who had a serene smile on his face, and dragged the former doctor away.

Dr. Boyd smiled to himself. He had finally done it; he had beaten Dr. Olive. Their rivalry went back to medical school.

They had competed for everything: the best grades, the best internships; but before any of the medical stuff, there was Sarah. That's really where the whole competition thing started—with a girl they both liked. Sarah was doing her residency at Walter Hospital, the same hospital where both he and Frank were doing their residencies. They both did everything they could to impress her. They bought her flowers, candy, clothes, anything they could think of to win her over. At first it seemed like she was keener on him, but Dr. Olive had eventually won her over.

It killed him to see her with him; and the worst part of it was that he knew that Frank didn't even love her, at least not the way he did. One night the two of them were coming home from a party and were in a car accident. A drunk driver plowed right into them. Frank got out of it with only a broken arm, but Sarah died a few hours later in the hospital. He blamed Frank for her death and not the driver because she shouldn't have been with him in the first place.

I would have protected her; I would never have let anything happen to her, he thought.

Frank took the job here at Looney Bin Incorporated just to keep up the competition. He really didn't have a grudge against Dr. Boyd; he just saw it as a challenge, as a bit of fun. It was more than that for Dr. Boyd. He saw it as a war, a war that he had just won.

Chapter 34

Nurse Lovington was in love with Dr. Mannequin Olive. She couldn't help it; with his boyish hair cut, pleasing smile and sophisticated glasses, he was irresistible. She started fixing her hair and wearing eyeliner, and she bought more flattering shoes that didn't squeak.

She wasn't sure if he felt the same way about her or not; he was difficult to read. She had been flirting with him relentlessly; and although he seemed receptive, she felt insecure.

She decided to go into his office and talk to him about her feelings. He had finished seeing all his patients for the rest of the day, so he would be free. She was preparing herself for the worst, that he could be offended and/or outraged. He could demand her immediate dismissal.

*If that's what he wants, then so be it; but I just can't keep these feelings bottled up any more, s*he thought.

For once, she walked down the hall to his office without squeaking. She didn't bother knocking; she was on a mission and determined not to be dismissed. When she walked in, she wished she had knocked.

Sitting on Dr. Mannequin Olive's lap was Isabella the cook, and she was kissing Dr. Mannequin Olive. He seemed to be enjoying it a great deal.

Isabella startled, leaped off his lap and nearly landed on her butt.

"Nurse Lovington, I didn't hear you come in. I was just asking Dr. Mannequin Olive if he wanted anything special for lunch today," Isabella said.

"Like what? Your tongue?" Nurse Lovington said.

She leaped over Dr. Mannequin Olive's desk like an Olympic high jumper and grabbed Isabella around the neck. Isabella struggled with Nurse Lovington's hands, but she couldn't remove the iron grip she had around her neck, so she kicked Nurse Lovington in the shin, which loosened her grip; and then she headbutted her.

Nurse Lovington staggered back, and blood began to flow from her nose.

"You bitch!" Nurse Lovington yelled.

Nurse Lovington slapped Isabella across her face.

Dr. Mannequin Olive was wisely staying seated and not interfering with the two women. As a doctor, he was not going to take sides; he would remain neutral. A good doctor never makes judgments.

The two were knocking papers over and making such a racket that they didn't hear or notice Potbelly come in.

"What is going on? Stop it, you two," Potbelly said.

Neither of them paid the least bit attention to Potbelly; they kept right on fighting.

Nurse Lovington got Isabella in a head lock but let go after Isabella yanked a lock of her hair out. There was screaming and scratching and slapping and slamming. It was pure pandemonium.

Isabella picked up the vase on Dr. Mannequin Olive's desk and hurled it at Nurse Lovington. Nurse Lovington moved out of the way, and it hit Potbelly in the head. Isabella and Nurse Lovington watched as he dropped to the floor. Isabella, terrified, ran out of the office. Nurse Lovington raced over to Potbelly's limp body and checked for a pulse. It was slow but steady, as if he were asleep. She cradled his head in her hands.

Nurse Lovington burst into tears and pointed to Dr. Mannequin Olive, who seemed completely unfazed by it all.

"This is your fault. Why did you have to go and kiss that tramp? Well, don't just sit there; say something," she said.

Nurse Lovington looked at Dr. Mannequin Olive. He was so handsome and confident, and she felt like a fool. Isabella was kissing him, after all, not the other way around.

"You do care for me; I knew you did. I knew that I wasn't the only one who felt this way," Nurse Lovington said.

She jumped up to throw herself in Dr. Mannequin Olive's arms; and as she did, Potbelly's head slid off her hands and hit the floor.

"Oh, Dr. Mannequin Olive," she said as she smothered him in kisses.

When Potbelly finally woke up, he had a splitting headache.

"What happened?" he groaned.

He looked around; he was in Dr. Mannequin Olive's office, but there was no Dr. Mannequin Olive, no Nurse Lovington and no Isabella. Everything had been put back in its proper place. All the papers were in a neat pile on top of his desk.

I must have walked in on a love triangle, Potbelly thought.

He put his hand on top of the hardback chair next to him for support and hoisted himself up to a standing position.

"That is the second time I've been knocked out in this office,"

Potbelly said aloud.

Potbelly staggered into the dayroom. Crazy Bob noticed him wobbling and called him over to where he and Drake were seated. It was their free hour in the dayroom, and Lester was jumping about the room; he called it interpretative dance. Everyone else thought he looked like a mime, minus the painted face. Godot was wearing a dress and a top hat. He had not found his clothes yet, so Nurse Lovington let him borrow a dress of hers until they turned up. Virgil wasn't in the dayroom; he was in his own room, hard at work on the wax figure head of the other prominent Virgil. Fritz and Abram were playing poker, arguing over a hand.

"Had a little too much to drink?" Crazy Bob asked.

"No, I was knocked out in Dr. Mannequin Olive's office," Potbelly said.

"Dr. Mannequin Olive knocked you out?" Drake asked, surprised.

"No, Isabella did with a vase," Potbelly said.

"Why would Isabella want to knock you out with a vase?" Crazy Bob asked.

"I would have gone for something surefire if I were trying to knock someone out, like his stapler or that owl clock that sits on his desk," Drake said.

"Isabella wasn't trying to knock me out; she was trying to knock out Nurse Lovington," Potbelly said.

"Why would Isabella want to knock out Nurse Lovington?" Crazy Bob asked.

"They were fighting when I came into Dr. Mannequin's office. I think I might have walked in on a *ménage a trois*," Potbelly said.

"You walked in on them speaking French?" Crazy Bob asked.

"No, I mean I think it was a threesome that went wrong somehow," Potbelly said.

"There's no such thing as a threesome going wrong," Crazy Bob said.

"I think maybe he means there is some kind of love triangle between Dr. Mannequin Olive, Isabella and Nurse Lovington," Drake said.

"A love triangle is just like the Bermuda triangle; someone is going to get sucked into a strange vortex and never seen again," Crazy Bob said.

"I don't know; all I know is that they were scratching, punching and clawing at each other. Would you believe that Dr. Mannequin Olive didn't even try to stop it?" Potbelly said.

"Dr. Mannequin Olive is a stud," Drake said.

"Who won the fight?" Crazy Bob said.

"I don't know; when I woke up, everyone was gone," Potbelly said.

"You know now that you mention it, it's well past lunch time; and Isabella hasn't prepared anything. Also, Nurse Lovington hasn't dispensed medications yet today. I don't know about Dr. Mannequin Olive; I haven't seen him around lately," Crazy Bob said.

"I suspect foul play," Potbelly said.

"What kind of foul play?" Drake asked.

"The foulest kind," Potbelly said.

"Can you be more specific?" Crazy Bob asked.

"No, not really," Potbelly said.

"I suggest we split up and look for the three of them. I will look for Nurse Lovington. Drake, you look for Isabella; and, Potbelly, you look for Dr. Mannequin Olive," Crazy Bob said.

"What do you think happened to them?" Drake asked.

"I don't know, but I'm sure it's foul," Potbelly said.

Chapter 35

Drake got his magnifying glass and a note pad and pencil, so that he could look for clues like Sherlock Holmes. He wished he had a deerstalker hat so that he could better look the part of a master detective.

When he walked into the kitchen, Sam and Abram were there making themselves sandwiches.

"What are you guys doing?" Drake asked.

"Eating bread, so we won't be dead," Sam said.

"I was starving, so I came in here to ask Isabella when lunch would be ready. I didn't see her, so I decided to make myself a tuna salad sandwich," Abram said.

Drake put his magnifying glass up to Abram's face. He didn't see anything suspect other than an obscene amount of nose hair, so he jotted that down in his notebook.

"Was that before or after you murdered Isabella?" Drake asked.

"It was before. Wait. What?" Abram asked.

Drake had watched enough detective shows to know it was a good strategy to put suspects on the defensive; that way they will slip up and make a mistake.

"I said, 'Did you come in the kitchen to make yourself a tuna salad sandwich before or after you murdered Isabella?'" Drake asked.

"Isabella is dead?" Abram asked.

"So it would seem," Drake said.

Sam dropped his sandwich on the floor.

"Why does it seem like she's dead?" Abram asked.

"Because she's not here, and you had a motive for killing her," Drake said.

"What motive?" Abram asked.

"She would never serve any soda, only water, juice or milk, because she thought soda was bad for us. That just ate you up with anger. You couldn't stand it any longer, so boiling with white-hot rage, you killed her," Drake said.

Sam picked his sandwich up off the floor and continued eating.

"Where is her body?" Abram asked.

"We don't know; we haven't recovered a body," Drake said.

"Who is *we*?" Abram asked.

"Me, Crazy Bob and Potbelly," Drake said.

131

"Well, if you haven't found a body, how do you know she is dead?" Abram asked.

"She is missing and presumed dead. We suspect foul play," Drake said.

"What kind of foul play?" Abram asked.

"All kinds," Drake said.

"How long has she been missing?" Abram asked.

"A few hours," Drake said.

"So you think I killed Isabella just because she didn't give me any soda. Are you crazy?" Abram asked.

"Well, of course, I'm crazy; why else do you think I would be the top performer for Looney Bin Incorporated in craziness for five straight quarters in a row, right behind Crazy Bob," Drake said.

"What is Looney Bin Incorporated?" Abram asked.

Drake pointed down.

"This is Looney Bin Incorporated," Drake said.

"Do you mean the kitchen or are you pointing down further to hell?" Abram asked.

"I do not like hell; it is very hot. I do not like hell; it is a bad spot," Sam said.

"Both of them; it's all Looney Bin Incorporated,"

"Isabella is not here because she had a big fear," Sam said.

"Where did she go? What kind of fear?" Drake asked.

Sam shrugged his shoulders. He always shrugged his shoulders when he couldn't think of a rhyme.

Drake turned his magnifying glass on Sam, and it startled him so bad that he squeaked and dropped his tuna salad sandwich on the floor again with a splat.

"Oh no, my sandwich is down. My sandwich is down on the ground," Sam said.

"What Sam means is that she left because she was afraid she was going to be deported," Abram said.

"How do you know that?" Drake asked.

"Because she said so in the letter she left."

Abram showed him the letter on the counter.

Drake examined it through his magnifying glass; but it made the letters so big, he couldn't make it out, so he put the magnifying glass down and read it aloud.

To everyone,

I accidentally killed Potbelly today by throwing a vase at his head. I left because I was afraid of being deported back to my country. I will live a life on the run now, forever looking over my shoulder.

Sincerely,
Isabella
P.S.
Help yourselves to bread and tuna salad in the kitchen.

"I didn't know Isabella was from a foreign country," Drake said.
"She was; read the back," Abram said.
Drake flipped the letter over.

P.S.S.
Yes, I am a foreigner from a foreign country.

"Is Potbelly really dead?" Abram asked.
"No, Isabella only knocked him out with the vase," Drake said.
"That's a relief. I'm still getting over the death of Joseph, and I can only grieve over one person at a time," Abram said.
Crazy Bob and Potbelly came bursting through the kitchen, each of them holding a letter. Crazy Bob was waving it around like a crazy man.
"I know what happened to Nurse Lovington. She eloped with Dr. Mannequin Olive," Crazy Bob said.
"What does eloped mean?" Drake asked.
"I don't know, but it doesn't sound very good. If I had access to the interwebs, maybe I could goggle it," Crazy Bob said.
"Do you know how to goggle something?" Potbelly asked.
"Of course, I taught at Vanderbilt, for crying out loud," Crazy Bob said.
"Read the letter," Abram said.

Dear Patients and Staff:
I have eloped with Dr. Mannequin Olive. We are very much in love and going to start our lives new. I will cherish each and every one of you and think of you fondly.

Love,
Nurse Lovington

133

"Is that it? Is there a postscript?" Drake asked.
Crazy Bob turned the letter over.

P.S.
I have nothing further to say.

"I will miss Nurse Lovington. Whenever I think of a squeaky shoe, I will think of her," Abram said.
"How am I supposed to get a pot-bellied pig now?" Potbelly asked.
"What's your letter from Dr. Mannequin Olive say?" Drake asked.
"It looks like Nurse Lovington's hand. I guess she probably wrote it for him. Dr. Mannequin Olive was a man of few words," Potbelly said.
Potbelly read the letter to the group, who were brimming with curiosity, except for Sam, who was cutting himself a slice of pie he found in the refrigerator.

Dear Patients and Staff:
I have gone away to marry my beautiful, intelligent, sophisticated, erotic, exciting, classy, interesting and kind-hearted Felicia Lovington. I will never forget you and the time we've spent together.

Love always,
Dr. Mannequin Olive

"So Nurse Lovington has eloped with Dr. Mannequin Olive; and Dr. Mannequin Olive has married some girl named Felicia," Crazy Bob said.
"Felicia is Nurse Lovington's first name," Abram said.
"I thought Nurse Lovington's first name was Nurse," Crazy Bob said.
"Who's going to write a subscription for my medication?" Drake asked.
"Oh, I forgot to read the rest of it," Potbelly said.

P.S.

Drake can handle all of my patient's prescriptions through his placebo company.

"Yes, I can do that," Drake said with a smile.

"What happened to Isabella?" Crazy Bob asked.

"She thought she killed Potbelly with a vase, so she ran off for fear she might be deported because she was a foreigner," Drake said.

"What foreign country was Isabella from?" Potbelly asked.

"I don't know, probably one of those really foreign countries like Canada," Drake said.

"Do you think she is behind the plot to deprive Abram of his sodas and kill the queen of England?" Potbelly asked.

"She could have been a Canadian sleeper agent; only Lester would know," Drake said.

"Why would Isabella want to deprive me of soda, and why would she want to kill the queen of England?" Abram asked.

"We are currently fighting a Cold War with Canada. I don't know about the queen of England; that's classified," Crazy Bob said.

"With Nurse Lovington, Dr. Mannequin Olive and Isabella gone and Dr. Olive being in solitary confinement, who is in charge of Looney Bin Incorporated?" Potbelly asked.

"I guess that would be Dr. Boyd and the other board members," Drake said.

"Well, isn't this some fine piece of detective work we've done, boys?" Crazy Bob said.

Sam was finally done eating.

"I have finished all my pie. I'm afraid it's time to say goodbye," Sam said.

Sam exited the kitchen but left behind a trail of pie crumbs that fell from his shirt.

"What do we do now?" Drake asked.

"We eat," Crazy Bob said.

Chapter 36

Virgil had finished making the poet Virgil's head out of wax. He carried it into the dayroom under his arm. He saw Crazy Bob, Drake and Potbelly shooting the breeze in their usual spot.

Virgil pulled the other more prominent Virgil's head from underneath his arm pits and presented it to the group.

"What do you think? I think it's my greatest work to date," Virgil said.

"That is amazing; it looks just like him." Crazy Bob said even though he had no idea what the real Virgil looked like.

"You know, it's funny; but the moment I completed him, I've had an overwhelming desire to write," Virgil said.

"I knew you would; you just needed some inspiration," Crazy Bob said.

"You could write a sequel to *Inferno*," Drake said.

"Virgil didn't write *Inferno*; he was in the story, though," Crazy Bob said.

"You could call it *Return to Hell*," Potbelly said.

"That's a good idea, but I haven't read the original," Virgil said.

"I have a copy of the book if you want to read it, but I don't think it matters; you can write it however you want to. It doesn't have to be anything like the original. You could make it completely different. Have someone else go through hell besides Dante; maybe you could put yourself in it," Crazy Bob said.

"It might get confusing if Virgil goes through hell led by another Virgil," Potbelly said.

"Virgil doesn't have to lead him through hell; in fact, he should have someone more recent lead him through hell, someone that people these days would know," Crazy Bob said.

"You could lead him through hell, Crazy Bob," Drake said.

"No, it needs to be someone everyone knows; besides, it should also be someone who is dead," Crazy Bob said.

"Oh, I know. Joseph could lead him through hell," Potbelly said.

"No, that's not a good idea, because not everyone knew Joseph; and besides, he was invisible. I don't think anyone would want to read about an invisible man in hell," Crazy Bob said.

"Do you think Joseph is in hell?" Drake asked.

"No, I doubt it. It's pretty hard to torture someone you can't see,"

Crazy Bob said.

"I think you should change things around. You could be a realtor selling real estate in hell," Potbelly said.

"I bet the property values in hell are pretty low," Drake said.

"It probably just depends on where in hell the property is, because it's all about location," Crazy Bob said.

Fritz walked over to look at the wax Virgil.

"Das ist very gut. Can you make one of de Fuhrer?" Fritz asked.

"I don't do anti-Semites," Virgil said.

"What's an anti-Semite?" Potbelly asked.

"It means you don't like Semites," Crazy Bob said.

"Oh, what's a Semite?" Potbelly asked.

"They're a rock band from the 1970s," Crazy Bob said.

Abram burst through the dayroom screaming.

"Abram, you really have to stop screaming every time you don't get a soda; it's a little juvenile," Crazy Bob said.

"I'm not screaming because I didn't get a soda. I'm screaming because Dr. Olive is dead. He killed himself in solitary confinement," Abram said.

"How did he kill himself?" Drake asked.

"He hung himself with the string from the disco ball that Nurse Lovington used for Crazy Bob's party," Abram said.

"He pulled the string out from the disco ball and hung himself?" Crazy Bob asked.

"No, he didn't pull the string out; he just used it as a noose, so he hung himself right along with the disco ball," Abram said.

"That's original; I would have just used a shoe string or rope," Abram said.

"It's not that original; the Bee Gees died the same way," Crazy Bob said.

"Why did he kill himself?" Potbelly asked.

"There was a note attached. Dr. Boyd removed it, along with the body, but not before I had a chance to see it," Abram said.

"What did it say?" Drake asked.

"I can't remember all of it, but it said Looney Bin Incorporated was an evil corporation that exploited its employees," Abram said.

"How can we be employees? We never receive a pay check," Potbelly asked.

"Most big corporations do that; it's how they keep overhead down," Crazy Bob said.

"If we are employees, shouldn't we be doing some work?" Abram asked.

"I don't think that's in my job description," Crazy Bob said.

"We do work; it's our insanity that keeps this place in business," Drake said.

"Really? I must be one hell of a worker," Crazy Bob said.

"You are the top performer every quarter," Drake said.

"That's good; I wouldn't want to lose my job in this economy and have to go back to teaching at Dartmouth," Crazy Bob said.

"Are we being exploited like Dr. Olive said?" Potbelly asked.

"Yes, we are being exploited for our illnesses," Drake said.

"What can we do about it?" Abram asked.

"There's only one thing to do in a situation like this," Drake said.

"What's that?" Abram asked.

"We go on strike," Drake said.

"I don't think I can go on strike; I'm not that great of a bowler," Crazy Bob said.

"You don't have to bowl; you just have to not be crazy for the duration of the strike," Drake said.

"We should tell everyone at the next group meeting that we plan to go on strike," Abram said.

"Do we not act crazy starting now?" Drake asked.

"No, will start after we tell everyone," Potbelly said.

"Good, because I want to go paint faces on eggs," Drake said.

"What does a strike accomplish?" Crazy Bob asked.

"The company will lose money because its workers are refusing to work," Drake said.

Chapter 37

Everyone was gathered in the dayroom. Normally Nurse Lovington would be leading the meeting or circle time, as it was fondly known; but since her absence, it was sort of a free forum where anyone could stand up and speak.

Potbelly, Drake and Crazy Bob all stood up. The group quieted down in anticipation of some important announcement from the three seniors of Looney Bin Incorporated.

"Today we want to address a very important matter. Did you know that 50% of pot-bellied pigs that are taken as pets are abandoned every year?" Potbelly said.

Crazy Bob nudged him and shook his head.

"The strike," he whispered.

"Oh yes, today we want to talk to you about striking," Potbelly said.

"Yes, somebody needs to strike a match because Fritz farted," Abram said.

"Nein, I did not fart," Fritz said.

"Not strike a match; it's a different kind of strike," Potbelly said.

Everyone looked up with a combination of fascination and complete and utter bewilderment.

"What my esteemed colleague means is that we are planning on going on a strike. A strike is where everyone ceases to work until their demands are met," Drake said.

"Vut vork are ve zeazing to do?" Fritz asked.

"We are ceasing to be crazy from now on until our demands are met; we are to act completely normal," Drake said.

"What are our demands?" Lester asked.

"We don't have any at this time," Potbelly said.

"Actually, we do. We want Looney Bin Incorporated to stop being evil and to start paying us," Drake said.

"Paying us for what?" Lester asked.

"For being crazy," Drake said.

"But I'm not crazy," Abram said.

"Yes, you are, or you wouldn't be working for Looney Bin Incorporated," Drake said.

"I'm not really an employee here. I'm mostly in solitary confinement, so I'm technically more of an intern," Virgil said.

"In order for this to work, we are going to need 100%

participation, regardless of whether you're an employee, intern, temp or whatever," Drake said.

"Now we'll need a slogan. Does anyone have any ideas?" Crazy Bob asked.

"No dough, no go," Sam said.

"That's excellent, Sam. We will use that as our mantra," Crazy Bob said.

"But how will we stop being crazy? I don't how to be sane," Godot said.

Godot was still wearing Nurse Lovington's dress that she had given him before she left and a bag to match his shoes.

"For starters, you will have to start wearing normal clothes and put away that top hat," Crazy Bob said.

Godot gasped and took off his top hat and hugged it close to him with affection.

"I know we will all have to make sacrifices, but it's for our own good," Drake said.

"Once we start acting sane, their stock will begin to plummet; and they will meet our demands," Drake said.

"It won't be easy; and we will have to take baby steps, but I believe we can persevere," Crazy Bob said.

"Now I'm going to address each one of you and tell you what you must stop doing immediately," Drake said.

"Godot, you will need to wear clothes from now on and stop keeping people waiting for you all the time," Drake said.

Godot sighed and looked down. He didn't say anything; he only nodded his head in acquiescence.

"Abram, you will have to stop screaming every time you don't get your way," Drake said.

Abram started to scream, but Drake cut him off.

"Starting now, Abram," Drake said.

"Lester, you need to stop creeping around like a CIA operative and walk normally," Drake said.

Lester looked surprised.

"I don't creep around," Lester said.

"Yes, you do," Drake said.

"Oh, no one ever said anything before," Lester said.

"Fritz, you need to take off that swastika and no more goose-stepping or talking about the Fuhrer," Drake said.

"Nein. Nein. Nein," Fritz said.

"Ja. Ja. Ja," Drake said.

Fritz took off his swastika and removed the iron cross that was pinned to his lapel.

"Sam, you will need to stop rhyming and speak like a normal person," Drake said.

Sam shook his head vigorously.

"If you need to speak, just say our mantra. It rhymes and it won't sound crazy," Drake said.

Sam nodded his head, appeased.

"Crazy Bob, everyone is to now call you Robert. You are to stop elaborating and embellishing. Potbelly, everyone is to call you Richard; and you are to stop talking about pot-bellied pigs. Now that leaves me. I have to stop painting faces on eggs. I will still be selling placebos, though, because that's not crazy; that's capitalism," Drake said.

"Dr. Boyd is the only doctor on staff now, so when you have your sessions, try to act completely normal. If you need a visual aid, start watching the T.V here in the dayroom," Drake said.

"Does everyone understand what to do?" Robert asked.

Half the group nodded in the affirmative, and the other half shook their heads in the negative.

"Good, because we start right now," Drake said.

Chapter 38

Sam was sweating and fidgeting in his chair.

"Are you feeling okay, Sam?" Dr. Boyd asked.

"No dough, no go," Sam said.

"You've been saying that throughout our session, but what does it mean?" Dr. Boyd asked.

"No dough, no go," Sam said.

Patient is incoherent and crazier than ever, afraid it may be early onset of dementia, Dr. Boyd wrote.

"Okay, Sam, you can go now. I'll see you next week at the same time," Dr. Boyd said.

"No dough, no go," Sam said.

"I know, Sam; you run along now," Dr. Boyd said.

When Sam left Dr. Boyd's office, he was sweating so bad that he had sweat stains around his armpits. He bumped into Robert, formerly known as Crazy Bob.

"Hi, Sam, did you let Dr. Boyd know about our strike?" Robert asked.

"No dough, no go," Sam said in a hysterical voice.

"Yes, that's it exactly. You've done well, my friend," Robert said.

Robert went inside Dr. Boyd's office and sat down.

Dr. Boyd was busy writing something down and didn't see Robert walk in. After a few minutes of just sitting there, Robert cleared his throat.

"Hi, Robert, I didn't see you there. Are you ready to get started?" Dr. Boyd asked.

"Yes," Robert said.

"Last time we spoke, you said the stink bugs that were in your room flew into your ear while you were sleeping; and now they are controlling your mind," Dr. Boyd said.

Robert thought about that. It was hard to know if that sounded crazy or not. It was true. The stink bugs had invaded his brain and were putting thoughts into his head; but whatever he said in the past must have been crazy, he reasoned, so from now on he would just say the opposite of what he had said in the past.

"No, I wasn't feeling well last time we spoke. There are no stink bugs in my head. I have just a normal, average head, without any stink bugs, just like everyone else," Robert said.

"Are you sure because you said the stink bugs were telling you to kill your wife?" Dr. Boyd asked.

Robert had to think really hard about that one. He often got confused about whether his wife was still living or if she were dead. He went with the latter.

"My wife has been dead for a number of years," Robert said.

"Yes, that's right, your wife is dead. Do you know how she died?"

Robert began to panic. He couldn't remember how she had died; it was all a blur.

"I don't feel like talking about that right now; it's still too painful," Robert said.

Dr. Boyd seemed to accept this answer and changed topics.

"Does your head feel okay, I mean besides having stink bugs in it? Have you had any more headaches?" Dr. Boyd asked.

Dr. Boyd seemed determined to get him to admit that his head had been invaded by stink bugs, which they had; and at this very moment, the stink bugs were telling him to fart on Dr. Boyd.

Robert, who had eaten a tuna fish sandwich with olives right before their meeting, lifted his leg and let one rip.

"Excuse me," Robert said.

Dr. Boyd was careful not to let his facial expression change even when the odor wafted under his nostrils; he was a professional, after all.

"You were saying—" Dr. Boyd said.

"I was saying perfectly sane things," Robert said.

"What perfectly sane things?" Dr. Boyd asked.

"You know, about me having a perfect head, not invaded by stink bugs," Robert said.

"I see. Are you sure you're feeling okay?" Dr. Boyd asked.

"Yes, I feel perfectly sane, as sane as when I was teaching…"

He stopped. He almost said as sane as when he taught at UCLA, but he remembered that was something he talked about in the past.

"Yes, yes, you were saying about teaching?" Dr. Boyd asked.

"I was going to say as sane as when I used to teach Sunday school," Robert said.

Dr. Boyd raised an eyebrow.

"You never told me you taught Sunday school. I thought you believed in absurdism?" Dr. Boyd said.

"Once upon a time I taught Sunday School," Robert said.

"So you never taught as a professor?" Dr. Boyd said.

"Correct, I was never a professor," Robert said.

"I've never heard you admit that before; you've always stood by your claim that you were an English professor," Dr. Boyd said.

Robert laughed nervously; like Sam, he was starting to sweat profusely. Trying to appear sane was taking a lot out of him.

"What's so funny?" Dr. Boyd asked.

"Oh, just the fact that you thought I had been an English professor," Robert said.

"Clearly my mistake," Dr. Boyd said.

Dr. Boyd eyed him skeptically.

"Are you taking your medications?" Dr. Boyd asked.

"Yes, every day," Robert said.

"That's good, Robert. Now I had one last question about stink bugs," Dr. Boyd said.

"There are no stink bugs; I saw them when I was delusional. I was clearly insane at the time, but I'm not insane now; I am the opposite of insane," Crazy Bob yelled.

"Okay, Robert, don't get excited," Dr. Boyd said.

"I'm not excited. Do I look excited to you?" Robert asked.

"You don't seem like your usual self," Dr. Boyd said.

"Damn it, man, I'm not my usual self; my usual self is insane, and I am perfectly sane. I keep telling you that," Robert said.

"Are you working too hard?" Dr. Boyd asked.

Robert tensed at the word "working" and nearly jumped out of his seat.

"Work? What do you mean work? What kind of work?" Robert asked.

"I mean, are you trying too hard to act normal because you think that is what is expected of you?" Dr. Boyd asked.

"Don't be ridiculous. I'm not working; it's not like I work for an evil corporation or something," Robert said.

After he said it, he clasped his hand over his mouth because he felt he had revealed too much.

Dr. Boyd frowned.

"Is the death of Dr. Olive bothering you?" Dr. Boyd asked.

"Well, yes. I mean, how could it not? It was very tragic even though I didn't know him that well," Robert said.

"What prompted you to say 'evil corporation' just now?" Dr. Boyd asked.

"No reason, it just popped into my head," Robert said.

"Like the stink bugs just popped into your head," Dr. Boyd said.

"Yes, I mean no," Robert said.

"Well, which is it?" Dr. Boyd asked.

"It's no," Robert said.

"Why are you agitated?" Dr Boyd asked.

"Because you keep trying to get me to say that there are stink bugs in my head, and I already told you that they are not," Robert said.

Not only were the stink bugs in his head, they were also making a buzzing sound in his ear; and they were telling him to fart again because that is what they did in distress.

Robert jumped out of his chair.

"I believe our time is up," Robert said.

"We have another ten minutes," Dr. Boyd said.

Robert wasn't wearing a watch, but he looked at his arm and pointed to it like he was wearing one.

"Nope, time is up," Robert said.

He ran out of the door before Dr. Boyd could comment.

Dr. Boyd ran his hand through his hair and wrote some notes.

Patient is very agitated, having delusions that he is sane. Conclusion: Bat shit crazy. Recommend increase in medication.

Chapter 39

Dr. Boyd sat at his desk and smiled to himself. He enjoyed being the only doctor on staff. With Doctor Olive dead and Doctor Mannequin Olive gone god-knows-where with Nurse Lovington, he was 100% in charge. After seeing all the patients this week, he was very pleased at the trend he was finding. It seems that all the patients were trying to pass themselves off as sane for some reason; no doubt it was some notion that Crazy Bob got into his head and convinced the others to go along with. The results were great, though, because the more the patients tried to convince him they were sane, the crazier they sounded. It was a wonderful paradox.

Godot had sat right down in his office in all of his clothes and pretended he never went around naked. So Dr. Boyd wrote down: *Patient is suffering from body dysmorphic disorder.*

Fritz pretended he wasn't a Nazi sympathizer, so Dr. Boyd wrote in his chart: *Patient has created a split personality.* Every patient now had a new diagnosis, in addition to their old one.

The insanity had quadrupled in one week. The stock holders were going to be very pleased about these numbers.

Dr. Boyd sighed. He was a little disappointed that Dr. Olive had killed himself. It seemed like his vendetta against Frank was what kept him going and gave him purpose; now it was over.

He didn't think the man would have given up so easily; he overestimated him. The competition that had started in school and continued on at Looney Bin Incorporated was now over.

Dr. Boyd reached into his desk and removed the suicide note that Dr. Olive had written. He took it, even though he knew it was wrong. His mother, Martha, should have been able to read it, but in it he condemned Looney Bin Incorporated as an evil corporation; and he didn't want anyone else to see it and inquire as to what it meant. Abram, though, must have looked at the note because he remembered Crazy Bob mentioning the words "evil corporation."

He read the note again.

Dear mother, friends & colleagues,
I love you all, except you, Dr. Boyd; you are a giant horse's ass.
Everything I love, everything that I am has been taken from me by Looney Bin Incorporated. I am now a patient in the very facility where I once treated people. All I ever wanted to be was a

psychiatrist and help people. Looney Bin Incorporated doesn't care about helping its patients to get better; it only cares about profits. They would rather see the patients sick than to lose money. I am ashamed to admit that I was ever caught up in it. My desire to beat Dr. Boyd at everything overshadowed my better judgment. Looney Bin Incorporated is an evil corporation, and it needs to be taken down. Mother, please know that I had to do this, even though I love you deeply. I am nothing without my work, and I couldn't face seeing your disappointment. Take care of yourself.

Love,
Frank Olive

P.S. Somebody water the plants in my office.

Dr. Boyd crumpled up the letter and put it into his ashtray. He took out his cigarette lighter and set the paper on fire. He watched it twist and shrivel up. Dr. Boyd watched as Dr. Olive's suicide note burned and along with it, the damaging accusations about the beloved Looney Bin Incorporated.

As he watched the paper turn to ash, he thought about Susan's funeral. It was a closed casket funeral; her body had gotten mangled in the car accident. All of her friends and family were there; and front and center was Frank Olive, who had come out of the accident unscathed, except for a broken arm. He stood there expressionless with a cast on his injured arm. Frank was neither weeping nor angry. He was angry, though; he was not angry at the drunk driver that had killed his beloved Susan, for he was dead too.

He was angry that Frank was alive and Susan wasn't. He searched his eyes for some sign of love, of a deep loss, the kind of loss he felt; but he saw nothing in those eyes.

He was convinced that Frank Olive had never really loved Susan; she was just another victory to him in there ongoing competition. That day he vowed he would beat Frank Olive at everything, not just the day-to-day trivial victories but at life; he would beat Frank Olive into the ground. He would find a way to destroy him.

He never spoke to Frank about Susan; he never let him know the hate he harbored in his heart for him. It was strange, now that Frank was dead, he had won; but it was a hollow victory. It didn't make him feel triumphant; it made him feel sad because what was he now?

Before, he was John Boyd, the man who hated Frank Olive, and now who was he? He had no wife, no children; his life was empty. He was nothing without his vengeance.

Chapter 40

Dr. Raven sent a camera crew to Looney Bin Inc. at the worst possible time. He was going to film a reality show. Everyone was pretending to be sane; and after about a week of no one doing anything crazy, they packed it up and decided that maybe crazy people weren't interesting after all. That didn't stop their profits from going up, though, thanks to Dr. Boyd's reports.

Drake showed everyone the next quarterly report.

"The company is doing better than ever," Potbelly said.

"What do we do now?" Crazy Bob asked.

"We go to plan B," Drake said.

"What was plan A?" Crazy Bob asked.

"Plan A was that we go on strike by acting sane so Looney Bin Incorporated would lose money," Drake said.

"That sounds like a good plan," Crazy Bob said.

"No dough, no go," Sam shouted.

"That's right, Sam. It didn't work; somehow, by acting sane, we must have appeared crazier than ever," Drake said.

"What is plan B?" Lester asked.

"Well, first thing is first: the strike is over. Everyone, you can go back to being crazy," Drake said.

Everyone clapped and cheered, Godot took off all of his clothes, Fritz put his swastika armband back on and Virgil dove under the table.

"Plan B is we are going to take over Looney Bin Incorporated in a hostile takeover," Drake said.

"I don't like violence," Abram said.

"Do you want me to call the agency, have someone take them out?" Lester asked.

"No, that won't be necessary. We won't be using any violence. A hostile takeover just means taking over the company, and we do that by buying up shares of stock. We need to get the word out to other patients at Looney Bin branches and have them buy up shares. Potbelly, call your cousin at the Looney Bin Incorporated in New York and let him know what we are doing," Drake said.

"Is this like buying a time share in a condo?" Potbelly asked.

"Well, kind of, only we won't be buying shares in a condo, we'll be buying shares in Looney Bin Incorporated so we can have controlling interest," Drake said.

"I'd rather have a condo," Lester said.

"Me too," Abram said.

"I tell you what, after we take over Looney Bin Incorporated, we'll get a time share in a condo," Drake said.

"My cousin Cow Paddy will spread the word; he's on the interwebs a lot. He started a social media sight; it's like Facebook, except it's for mental patients. It's called Crazybook," Potbelly said.

"Why is your cousin called Cow Paddy?" Virgil asked from underneath the table.

"He used to own a farm before he was committed, and he has an extensive collection of cow turds," Potbelly said.

"How du ve buy time zhares? I don't haf any money except for Reich marks," Fritz said.

"You all will become partners in my online placebo company, and we will expand," Drake said.

Crazy Bob raised his flannel shirt and looked at his stomach. "I'm already expanding," he said.

"Well, we will need to expand even further," Drake said.

"I don't get it," Potbelly said.

Crazy Bob patted him on the shoulder.

"It's okay; I know you didn't teach at MIT like some of us. Drake wants us to go into business with him and help him sell placebos, so that we can all buy more stock in Looney Bin Incorporated until we own enough shares to have controlling interest in the company. He also wants us to eat a lot so we can get really fat and expand," Crazy Bob said.

"I still don't get it," Potbelly said.

"It's a metaphor," Crazy Bob said.

"Okay, now I get it," Potbelly said.

"Let's get busy; we can do this," Drake shouted with enthusiasm.

"I huvn't zeen dis much pride in people zince der Fuhrer zpoke at Nuremburg," Fritz said and wiped a tear from his eye.

Chapter 41

Potbelly was on the phone in the dayroom with his cousin Cow Paddy. He didn't use the phone a whole lot; and he had it upside down, so he had to keep telling Cow Paddy to speak up because they had a bad connection.

"I need you to go on Crazybook and tell every patient you know to buy stock in Looney Bin Incorporated," Potbelly said.

"What are shares?" Cow Paddy asked.

"Did you say, what are sharks?" Potbelly asked.

"What are shares?" Cow Paddy asked again.

"I think they are like paper money, like in monopoly," Potbelly said.

"Why don't I just tell them to buy Monopoly shares; that would make more sense," Cow Paddy said.

"What? You have to speak up a bit; we seem to have a bad connection because I can barely hear you," Potbelly said.

"Why don't I just tell them to buy Monopoly shares? That would make more sense," Cow Paddy yelled.

"We won't be able to take control over Looney Bin Incorporated if we buy up Monopoly shares; we would be taking over the game Monopoly, and I don't want to do that because I always lose at that game," Potbelly said.

"Okay, I'll tell them to buy shares in Looney Bin Incorporated. Why do we want control over Looney Bin Inc. anyway?" Cow Paddy asked loudly.

"So we can get salaries, health benefits, 401K and vacation time, etc., the same things that a regular employee gets. We have been exploited for far too long," Potbelly said.

"What's exploited?" Cow Paddy asked loudly.

Potbelly just realized he had the phone upside down and turned it around.

"Why are you shouting? I can hear you just fine," Potbelly said.

"Sorry, I thought we had a bad connection. I asked what exploiters are," Cow Paddy said.

"You know exploiters, people who discover new things like Lewis and Clark and Columbus," Potbelly said.

"So what did we discover?" Cow Paddy asked.

"We discovered that we are crazy to work here under these conditions," Potbelly said.

151

"Okay, I'll see what I can do. I'm starting to turn a profit with Crazybook. I've gotten several calls from companies who want to pay me for advertising," Cow Paddy said.

"That's great. I'm partnering up with my friend Drake who sells placebos online," Potbelly said.

"What are placebos?" Cow Paddy asked.

"You know how regular medications always have side effects?" Potbelly asked.

"Yes, the one I'm on gives me bad diarrhea," Cow Paddy said.

"Placebos have no side effects; in fact, they have no effects at all," Potbelly said.

"Wow, a medication that has no effect! I'll take a hundred," Cow Paddy said.

"Great, I'll let Drake know; and we'll ship them right over at no charge since you're family," Potbelly said.

"So how's Aunt Theresa doing?" Cow Paddy asked.

"She's getting pretty senile. I told her I was getting married the last time she visited. She really wanted me to get married and have children; I couldn't stand to disappoint her."

She wouldn't understand that it's hard to meet someone when you're in a looney bin," Potbelly said.

"You should join Crazybook. Lots of people who've joined have found relationships, including me. I'm engaged to be married," Cow Paddy said.

"You're kidding me," Potbelly said.

"No and I'm sure you could find somebody too," Cow Paddy said.

"I'll go online today and join. We have a new computer in the dayroom. The FBI had to confiscate our old one because somehow Crazy Bob broke into their files. They thought he was a terrorist. Then after questioning him, they realized he wasn't a terrorist; he was just crazy. He kept asking them to waterboard him to make sure he wasn't a terrorist, and they kept refusing. I think Lester might have called them. He thinks everything is a Canadian plot," Potbelly said.

"I had no idea the Canadians plotted anything," Cow Paddy said.

"He seems to think they are constantly plotting to kill, marginalize or mildly annoy someone or something," Potbelly said.

"That sounds exciting; nothing exciting ever happens here. So, what are we going to do once we have control over Looney Bin

Incorporated?" Cow Paddy asked.

"The first thing I'm going to do is get a pot-bellied pig," Potbelly said.

"That's great. I remember the pot-bellied pigs you had growing up. One of them ate my homework; and when I told the teacher about it, she didn't believe me. She punished me for telling lies and gave me a zero on my homework," Cow Paddy said.

"Yeah, I remember that," Potbelly said.

"First thing I'm going to do is import foreign cow turds," Cow Paddy said.

"Cool, listen, I got to run; but I'll keep in touch," Potbelly said.

"Later, gator," Cow Paddy said.

Potbelly saw Crazy Bob, Drake and Virgil sitting at the usual table and walked over.

"I just talked to my cousin, Cow Paddy, and he's in. He's going to get everyone he knows to buy stock in Looney Bin Incorporated. Also, he wants to buy $100 of placebos," Potbelly said.

"Excellent. I'll put the order in," Drake said.

The Virgil wax head that Virgil had made was on the table, and Virgil the non-wax head was busy writing something down; and Crazy Bob was looking over his shoulder.

Crazy Bob had given up his attempt to write every conversation down. He decided he would live in the moment; and at this very moment, he was working on expanding and was gobbling down a bag of potato chips.

"What are you writing, Virgil?" Potbelly asked.

"I'm writing a short story. You know making this wax head of Virgil was a great idea; it's really inspired me," Virgil said.

"He's writing a story about a fictional character named Virgil who lives in Virginia and is a virgin; it's sensational so far," Crazy Bob said.

"I like the part about the guy named Virgil who lives in Virginia; I'm not sure about the virgin part," Potbelly said.

"What's wrong with virgins?" Drake asked.

"Well, I just mean sex sells, doesn't it?" Potbelly asked.

Crazy Bob thought back to the files he had discovered in the file room, the erotic fiction that Dr. Wells had written about Brad and Judy. It was pretty tantalizing, but he didn't think Dr. Wells had sold any of it.

"Not necessarily," Crazy Bob said.

153

"Can I see that?" Drake asked.

Virgil handed him the story.

"It's not finished yet, but you can read what I have so far," Virgil said.

"Hello, my name is Virgil, and I was born a virgin in Virginia," Drake read.

"It sounds really interesting so far," Potbelly admitted.

"Are you still planning to write a sequel to *Inferno*?" Drake asked.

"Oh, yes, I'm going to get around to that; but I have so many story ideas running through my head and so little time," Virgil said.

They heard yelling coming from the vending machine. Lester came running out.

"Abram did it; he finally got a soda from the soda machine," Lester said.

They all ran into the break room, and there Abram was lying on the floor; he was gulping down the soda so fast that it was running down his chin and neck. He had not only gotten one soda, it looked like he had gotten all the sodas in the entire machine.

"How did you get so many sodas?" Drake asked.

"I don't know. I just put in the usual 65 cents, expecting to get nothing; but then I heard one fall, so I grabbed it. Then the most amazing thing happened: another soda fell, then another, then another, until they all came out," Abram said.

"Do you realize what just happened? Your luck has finally changed; I think you just received sodas for all the times you've put in change and didn't get one," Crazy Bob said.

Abram just looked up and smiled; he was euphoric. He moved his arms and legs up and down like you do when you're lying in the snow and making snow angels, only he lacked coordination and couldn't move his arms and legs together at quite the same time. He was making crazy snow angels. The group left Abram in his triumph, and he lay there for the rest of the afternoon drinking sodas until his bladder finally made him get up and stagger to the bathroom.

Chapter 42

Crazy Bob was eating a candy bar; he had been expanding nicely. He had already added fifteen pounds to his staunch frame.

I'm coming along beautifully, he thought.

He spotted Potbelly at the computer and wobbled over to see what he was doing.

"Are you goggling pot-bellied pigs?" Crazy Bob asked.

"No, I'm setting up a profile on Crazybook," Potbelly said.

Crazy Bob looked at the picture of Potbelly. He had a wide grin, and his eyes were closed in it.

"When did you take this picture?" Crazy Bob asked.

"Just now, using the web cam," Potbelly said.

"It looks good," Crazy Bob said.

Crazy Bob read his profile.

Name: Richard Helen Thorton III, DOB: August 5ᵗʰ (no year given). POB: Trenton, NJ. School: Graduated from Hillsdale High School. Relationship status: It's complicated. Employment: It's very complicated. Religion: Atheist Catholic. Likes: Interested in pot-bellied pigs, talking to friends about pot-bellied pigs and women who like pot-bellied pigs.

"Your middle name is Helen?" Crazy Bob asked.

"Yes, after my father and his father," Potbelly said.

"Were they named Richard also?" Crazy Bob asked.

"No, my father's name was Trent, and my grandfather's name was Michael," Potbelly said.

"So what's the III after your last name?" Crazy Bob said.

"I'm the third Helen," Potbelly said.

"Maybe you should expand your interests a little further," Crazy Bob suggested.

Potbelly thought about that a moment before typing.

I am willing to talk on a limited basis about turtles.

"Hey, you have a friend request," Crazy Bob said.

Potbelly clicked on the friend request; he was a little disappointed because it was only his cousin, Cow Paddy. Cow Paddy was smiling the same toothy grin. They looked so much alike, they could have passed for siblings.

"Don't worry, you'll meet someone," Crazy Bob said.

Crazy Bob was eating a corn dog; he was determined to expand more than anyone else. Potbelly did not want to work on expanding, though, because he didn't think he would meet anyone if he expanded too much.

Drake walked into the dayroom. He hadn't got any fatter; but he had grown a beard, so he must be working on expanding his facial hair.

"Virgil is back in solitary confinement," Drake said.

"Why? He was really starting to come out of his shell. He was beginning to improve," Potbelly said.

"Yes, but that's it, isn't it? Looney Bin Incorporated doesn't want anyone to improve because they will lose money," Drake said.

"There's only one thing we can do," Crazy Bob said.

"I see where you're going with this. We need to break him out," Drake said.

"Actually, I was going to say that this corndog needs ketchup, but I like what you said better," Crazy Bob said.

"How do we get him out?" Drake asked.

"We'll need to get the key from Dr. Boyd's office, and we'll wait until everyone is asleep and bust him out," Potbelly said.

"That sounds risky," Drake said.

"Well, risky is my middle name," Potbelly said.

"I thought it was Helen," Crazy Bob said.

"If we get him out, we'll have to hide him; or Dr. Boyd will just put him right back in solitary confinement," Drake said.

"We'll have to get everyone to help us keep him out of sight," Crazy Bob said.

"You know, with Nurse Lovington, Dr. Olive, Dr. Mannequin Olive and Isabella gone, Dr. Boyd's stretched pretty thin. He is so busy micromanaging everything that I doubt he will even notice he's gone, at least for a while," Drake said.

"What's micromanaging?" Potbelly asked.

"It's where you manage everything yourself, even smaller tasks," Drake said.

"That's like Disney World; they manage the big world of Disney, and they also manage It's a Small World," Crazy Bob said.

"I've never been to Disneyworld," Potbelly said.

"I went once to the Apricot Center with my wife. We didn't see any apricots though. " Crazy Bob said.

"So do we understand the plan?" Drake asked.

"Yes, we are breaking Virgil out of solitary confinement and taking him to Disney World," Crazy Bob said.

"That sounds fun," Potbelly said.

"I'm going to micromanage this corndog some more," Crazy Bob said.

Chapter 43

Crazy Bob took Dr. Boyd's keys from underneath his snow globe just as he did when he broke into the file room. Drake had informed Godot, Sam, Fritz, Lester and Abram about their plan; and they all agreed to help. They were calling it Operation Aeneid after Virgil's famous epic poem. Only no one could pronounce Aeneid correctly, so it was Operation Antacid, Operation Annelid or Operation Anemone, depending on who was saying it. Sam couldn't think of anything to rhyme with Aeneid so he said nothing. It was to commence at 1300 hours, according to Drake; but no one knew what time that meant, so people were showing up at all hours in the dayroom. Finally at 3 a.m., after waiting on Godot, everyone was there so they got started.

They were each wearing camouflage except for Lester, who was wearing black spandex because he didn't have any camouflage, and Godot, who was naked and just wearing a beret on his head. Fritz had on a camouflage swastika armband. They each put shoe polish on their faces, as well, because they wanted to make sure they could blend in with their environment, which was mainly bright yellow walls and pastel colors.

"Okay, let's go over the check list," Drake said.

Crazy Bob pulled out the check list.

"Canteens. Check. Night vision goggles. Check. Ak-47 negative, I couldn't pass the background check. Duct tape. Check. Keys. Check. Cyanide capsules. Check. Pliers. Check. Kite. Check. Food provisions. Check. Spray paint. Check," Crazy Bob said.

"Vat is de zyanide capzulez vor?" Fritz asked.

"In case we're caught, and they try and get information out of us," Crazy Bob said.

"Where did you get them?" Lester asked.

"They are Drake's placebo cyanide capsules, so we won't really die," Crazy Bob said.

"What's the kite for?" Abram asked.

"In case we have to fly out of here," Crazy Bob said.

"Let's go over the plan," Drake said.

"We use Dr. Boyd's keys to get into Ward B. Then we spray paint the cameras with the spray paint. If there are any guards, Crazy Bob will take them out with karate and then duct tape them. We find Virgil and free him from his cell. We then take turns hiding him out in our rooms," Potbelly said.

"Then we have cake," Crazy Bob said.

"Sounds good; let's go," Drake said.

The crazy train proceeded down the hall toward Ward B. The lights were all turned out.

"Did we have a flashlight on that check list, Crazy Bob?" Potbelly asked.

"No, I forgot to put that on there," Crazy Bob said.

"Well, it's pitch black and I can't see a thing," Potbelly said.

"It's very dark here in the park," Sam said.

"We're not in a park, Sam," Potbelly said.

"Everyone, hold on to the person in front of you," Drake said.

"Someone is grabbing my butt," Lester said.

"Shhh, quiet!" Potbelly yelled.

"Godot, I think I grabbed your fingers," Abram said.

Abram tried to give Godot back his fingers but couldn't see his hands, so he put them in his pocket to return them later.

"Okay, I think this door is it," Crazy Bob said.

Crazy Bob tried all of the keys until one fit. When he opened the door, a mannequin fell out. Crazy Bob screamed and tried to do a karate kick on the mannequin; only he had grown too fat to lift his leg up very high, so instead he kicked Potbelly in the shin. Potbelly yelped.

"Shush!" Godot said.

"It's just the supply closet where we keep the mannequins," Drake said.

"Why do we have a supply closet with mannequins?" Lester asked.

"Where else are you supposed to keep your mannequins?" Crazy Bob said.

They went further down the hall until they came to another door. Crazy Bob tried a few keys before it opened. It was the entrance to Ward B. A stench hit them as soon as he opened the door; it was a strange odor, a confluence of moldy cheese, mouthwash and feces.

"Crazy Bob, did you cut the cheese?" Lester asked.

"I didn't bring any cheese," Crazy Bob said.

"No, it's just the smell in here; it's rancid," Drake said.

Crazy Bob came on a light switch and flicked it on. The ward was illuminated, and standing right in front of Crazy Bob was Virgil. It startled Crazy Bob. He kicked his leg out and missed, lost his footing and landed sprawled out on his back. Virgil, who was on his way to the bathroom, was equally startled and dove underneath the first thing he saw, which was a chair.

The night watchman came into the room.

"What is going on here?" the night watchman asked.

"Crazy Bob, duct tape him," Drake said.

Crazy Bob was still on the floor like a turtle on its shell; he was unable to get back up, and he had on the backpack with the supplies.

"Virgil, it'z uz, ve com to rezcue you," Fritz said.

"Germans have come to rescue me?" Virgil asked without poking his head out.

"No, it's us: Crazy Bob, Drake and the gang," Potbelly said.

"I'm calling Dr. Boyd," the night watchman said.

Abram pulled out one of Godot's fingers from his jacket and pointed it at him.

"You'll do no such thing," he said.

The night watchman saw the finger and looked terrified.

"Please don't hurt me. I have a pet goldfish at home, and I'm all he or she has," the night watchman said.

"No one is going to hurt you. Abram, give Godot back his fingers. We just want Virgil. Dr. Boyd put him in solitary confinement, and he needs to be with us," Crazy Bob said.

Crazy Bob was still lying on his back like a beached whale.

Abram gave Godot back his fingers.

"No, you've got it all wrong. I asked Dr. Boyd if I could be put back in solitary confinement for a while," Virgil said.

"Why would you want to be put back in solitary? Don't you like being on the outside with us?" Drake asked.

"The daily grind of Looney Bin Inc. can get too stressful for me, and sometimes I need a break," Virgil said.

"What about your writing?" Crazy Bob asked.

"I'm still going to write. Besides, I'm not totally alone; I still have the wax head of Virgil to keep me company with all his wisdom," Virgil said.

Sam started to cry.

"It is true. We miss you," he said.

"Don't cry, Sam; I'll be back before you know it," Virgil said.

The night watchman took pity on the crazy group of misfits.

"Look, if you all go back to your rooms and promise not to pull any more stunts like this, I promise I won't say anything to Dr. Boyd."

They each said goodbye to Virgil.

"Keep fighting the good fight, boys. I'll be back soon," Virgil said.

They left Ward B with their heads down in defeat. When they got back to the dayroom, they could see that the sun was coming up; it was almost time to start the day.

"I guess Operation Anorexia is a failure," Potbelly said.

"Speaking of anorexia, where's Crazy Bob?" Drake asked.

"Crazy Bob is anorexic?" Lester asked.

"No, he has the opposite of anorexia; he suffers from expansionism," Potbelly said.

They went back to Ward B to carry out Crazy Bob, who had fallen asleep on the floor.

Chapter 44

Crazy Bob wasn't crazy at the moment, which meant he was reading. He was reading *Catcher in the Rye* by J.D. Salinger.

"*Catcher in the Rye*—is that the movie about where they make a baseball field in the middle of a cornfield?" Drake asked.

"No, but a baseball field in the middle of a cornfield sounds like a good idea; it breaks up the monotony of just seeing corn for miles," Crazy Bob said.

"I'd like to play baseball in a cornfield," Potbelly said.

"This book is about a young man who just got kicked out of yet another boarding school, and he has a few days to kill before he is supposed to come home for Christmas break. It's a coming-of-age story, filled with prostitutes, pimps and the Christmas spirit," Crazy Bob said.

"I like prostitutes and pimps; I'm not so sure about the Christmas spirit," Drake said.

"Well, that's more in the background really. It's more about teenage angst and talking about how people are phony. He uses that word a lot to describe people," Crazy Bob said.

"What's a phony?" Potbelly asked.

"It's someone who isn't real," Crazy Bob said.

"You mean like Joseph?" Drake asked.

"No, Joseph was real; he was just invisible. I mean not real in the sense of not being genuine," Crazy Bob said.

"I know what you mean; I hate it when people wear fake leather," Potbelly said.

"Anyway, you have to be very careful with this book. You can't read it too many times, or you will become obsessed with it; and it will drive you to shoot someone," Crazy Bob said.

"Wow, really? I didn't know a book could tell you to shoot someone. How many people have shot someone?" Drake asked.

"At least three that I know of, one of them being John Lennon," Crazy Bob said.

"A book shot John Lennon?" Drake asked incredulously.

"Not the book, but a man carrying the book who was inspired by it," Crazy Bob said.

"A book inspired a man to shoot John Lennon. The Russians must have been really angry," Drake said.

"Not that Lennon, the other one, the one who was a walrus and lived in a yellow submarine," Crazy Bob said.

"They shot a walrus? That's just wrong," Potbelly said.

"I wished I lived in a yellow submarine too," Drake said.

"I wish I lived in a red one; all the walls here are yellow, and I'm tired of yellow quite frankly," Crazy Bob said.

"How are we doing at buying up shares?" Potbelly asked.

"Not so good; the company is larger than I thought. At this rate we could be buying them for years and not even putting a dent in it," Drake said.

"I've been trying my hardest to expand, but it looks like I've failed you," Crazy Bob said, patting his extensive gut.

"It's not your fault, Crazy Bob; we've just got to come up with another plan," Drake said.

"My mom always says when one door closes, another one will probably close too because our house was always so drafty," Potbelly said.

"What do we do if all the doors close?" Drake asked.

"Can we go out the window?" Crazy Bob asked.

"All the windows here are painted shut," Potbelly said.

"I know; we will fall through a trap door," Crazy Bob said.

"Good idea; we just have to find a trap door to this problem. That's a good metaphor, Crazy Bob," Drake said.

"What metaphor? I mean we literally need to start looking for a trap door," Crazy Bob said.

Drake, Crazy Bob and Potbelly spent the rest of the day looking for a trap door. They didn't find one, just a lot of dust, some gum wrappers, loose change and a condom. They were disappointed about not finding it; but when Crazy Bob looked behind the curtains in his room, he got an unexpected surprise.

There on the curtain, just sitting there minding its own business, was a stink bug.

Chapter 45

Time went by as it did in the looney bin, quickly but strangely. Virgil did continue to write; he finished his story, "Virgil the Virgin from Virginia." It had been published and was now number one on the New York Times bestselling list. Virgil was out touring and promoting his new book. This was difficult since he suffered from social anxieties and heard voices. At book signings, people would thrust their books underneath the table; and he would sign the book for them. Sometimes people wanted to ask him questions, so they had to get underneath the table with him. The wax head of Virgil went with him on every book signing.

Strangely enough, this did not hurt Virgil; people loved it. They thought he was just an eccentric genius. Virgil dedicated the book to the boys at Looney Bin Incorporated. Virgil's replacement was a patient named Max, but they hardly ever saw him. Max had such a severe case of OCD that he could hardly leave his room. He started his morning at 5:55 a.m.

If for some reason he slept through his alarm and did not get up at that exact time, he stayed in bed for the rest of the day and did not get up until the next morning at that time. Once he was up, he had to make up his bed; and if every corner wasn't tucked in just right, he pulled it out and started all over. If he managed to make it to breakfast, he had to chew each bite of food 100 times before swallowing it, which made talking to him impossible since he might lose count and have to start all over.

It felt like just another day at Looney Bin Incorporated until the gang got some surprise visitors.

Nurse Lovington strolled through the double doors carrying Dr. Mannequin Olive under one arm, and strapped around her waist and shoulders in a carrier was a baby. She wasn't in her nurse's attire, but she was wearing the squeaky white shoes.

Crazy Bob was the first to spot them.

"Look what the cat dragged in," he shouted.

Lester jumped about ten feet in the air; he hadn't noticed them.

"Oh my god, what cat? I'm allergic to cats," he said.

Crazy Bob pumped Dr. Mannequin's arm vigorously; then he pumped Nurse Lovington's hand vigorously; then he pumped the baby's hand vigorously.

The startled, sleeping baby let out a small cry.

"And who is this little person?" Crazy Bob asked.

"Her name is Olivia Olive," Nurse Lovington said.

Everyone came into the dayroom to see what all the commotion was except for Dr. Boyd, who was in a meeting.

They gazed at the happy family. They all had a dark tan, including the baby. They had obviously just come from someplace sunny.

"We just heard about Dr. Olive's suicide, so we wanted to come straight away," Nurse Lovington said.

"Look at dis baby; it lookz juzt like a little Fuhrer, with itz round red cheekz," Fritz said.

The baby took one look at Fritz and began to cry. Nurse Lovington slapped a pacifier in the baby's mouth to calm her down. The baby quieted down but kept a wary eye on Fritz.

"It was terrible; he hung himself with the disco ball we used at Crazy Bob's party," Abram said.

"This company is like hell. None of us are doing well," Sam said.

"Hello, Sam. I know, that's why we've come to see you guys," Nurse Lovington said.

"We have a plan, though; we are trying to purchase up shares of Looney Bin Incorporated. It's going really slow; it's such a huge corporation," Drake said.

"You need more money and we can help. That's why we've started our own company. It's called Insane in the Brain, and it's doing really well. We can help you purchase shares so you can take over Looney Bin Incorporated," Nurse Lovington said.

"Insane in the Brain; I like it," Potbelly said.

"All of our patients also own stock in the company, so they can profit share," Nurse Lovington said.

"That's great," Drake said.

"They also get paid and have health benefits," Nurse Lovington said.

"How are your patients?" Crazy Bob asked.

Nurse Lovington winked at him.

"They're good, but they're young; they don't have your expertise at being crazy," Nurse Lovington said.

That made Crazy Bob smile.

"We were afraid we would never see you again," Abram said.

"I know, but Dr. Mannequin Olive and I were so much in love and wanted to be together. We can't keep our hands off one another," she said.

165

She kissed Dr. Mannequin Olive on the lips and slapped him on the behind. It seemed as though Nurse Lovington was the one who was all hands; Dr. Mannequin Olive showed restraint, as was his nature.

"So we will join forces and take the company down," Drake said.

"Ja, vill be de Axiz powerz," Fritz said.

"The Axis powers lost, Fritz," Godot said.

"They did?" Fritz asked in surprise.

"We'll be the non-Axis powers. I will play the role of Churchill," Crazy Bob said.

Crazy Bob patted his stomach to indicate he was the only man fit to play a man of Churchill's stature.

The baby cooed at Crazy Bob's suggestion; it was all the confirmation they needed. They would be the non-Axis powers, and they were going to win this war.

Chapter 46

Potbelly was talking to his new girlfriend on Crazybook.

Her name was Lillian Edwina Rosenthal, but everyone called her Sue for no apparent reason.

He was on her profile page; he loved to read it over and over. In her profile picture, she was wearing her hair in braids in a bun on either side of her head like Princess Leia in Star Wars. Her face was covered in freckles; and she had a wide smile, which revealed a pair of buck teeth. She was not pretty by anyone's definition, but to Potbelly she was a goddess. She didn't know anything about pot-bellied pigs, but that didn't bother him because she listened enthusiastically when he talked about them. She sent him a direct message.

When can we be together, my love? Each day without you is like an eternity. Today we were forced to make baskets during arts and crafts time. It's like working in a sweatshop; I don't think I can endure it much longer. I had a dream about you. In my dream we lived on a farm and we had lots of pot-bellied pigs, cows and sheep. We had one great big pot-bellied pig which we called Big Pig II, named after the pet you once owned. We had ten children, all boys and all named Drake and Bob. It was such a lovely dream. I count the days until we can be together, my dearest.

Potbelly smiled; it was a nice dream. He would like to have ten children and live on a farm. The best thing of all was that he wouldn't have to lie to his mother anymore; he was finally going to get married. Sue worked for Looney Bin Incorporated too in Chicago.

Potbelly sent her a direct message.

My dearest Tulip, we will be together before you know it; but first I have to help my friends take over this evil corporation. We've got some old friends, a former nurse and doctor who used to work here, helping us; but I fear it may not be enough. Looney Bin Incorporated is a big bloated beast, like a pot-bellied pig that's eaten too many potatoes. I hope that our luck will change soon, and someone will come to our rescue.

Just as Potbelly typed that last line, the phone rang in the dayroom. Crazy Bob put his book down and waddled over to get it.

"Crazy Bob here; Crazy is my name and my game," he said.

"This is Cow Paddy. Is Potbelly there?" Cow Paddy asked.

"You want to sell cow paddies to Potbelly?" Crazy Bob asked.

"I want to speak to Potbelly," Cow Paddy said.

"I have a potbelly," Crazy Bob said and patted his tummy.

"No, I need to speak to my cousin Richard," Cow Paddy said.

"I don't think we have a cousin Richard here," Crazy Bob said.

Cow Paddy was becoming exasperated.

"I need to speak to the man who talks about pot-bellied pigs all the time; he's thin and has a receding hair line."

"Is there someone here who likes pot-bellied pigs, is thin and has a receding hair line?" Crazy Bob yelled out in the dayroom.

"That's me," Potbelly said.

"Me too," Lester said.

"We seem to have two people to fit that description," Crazy Bob said.

"You don't like pot-bellied pigs, Lester," Potbelly said.

"I do, kind of," Lester said.

"Not as much as me, and your hair line is not receding," Potbelly said.

"I went undercover once to infiltrate the mafia, and I wore a wig with a receding hair line," Lester said.

Potbelly grabbed the phone.

"This is Potbelly here," Potbelly said.

"Hey, Potbelly, it's Cow Paddy," Cow Paddy said.

"It's definitely for me," Potbelly yelled.

"Mystery solved," Crazy Bob said.

"I've got some great news. I've had an offer from someone who wants to buy Crazybook. There's a company that is willing to pay me two billion dollars," Cow Paddy said.

"Wow, in real money or Monopoly money?" Potbelly asked.

"I assume real money, but I'll have to get clarification on that. With that kind of money, I can buy up the remaining shares that we need to have controlling interest in Looney Bin Inc.," Cow Paddy said.

"That's great, Cow Paddy. I have some exciting news myself. Things are getting pretty serious between Sue and me; and now that the takeover looks promising, we are going to get married," Potbelly said.

"You dog, you. See, I told you all you needed to do was join Crazybook," Cow Paddy said.

"I'll send an invitation just as soon as we've set a firm date. I want you to be one of my groomsmen," Potbelly said.

"I would love that," Cow Paddy said.

When Potbelly got off the phone with his cousin, he looked around for Crazy Bob. He was still there, sitting at their usual table reading a book. Potbelly walked over to him; he tried to read the title, but Crazy Bob was holding the book upside down.

"I just got off the phone with Cow Paddy," Potbelly said.

"You just talked to a cow paddy? That must have been a fascinating conversation; I've always wondered what a cow paddy had to say," Crazy Bob said.

Potbelly sighed. He didn't feel like trying to explain who Cow Paddy was again; he had something more important he wanted to ask him.

"I'm going to be getting married," Potbelly said.

"You are going to marry the cow paddy? That was quick," Crazy Bob said.

"No, I'm getting married to a girl; and I want you to be my best man," Potbelly said.

"I was married once," Crazy Bob said.

"I know, Bob," Potbelly said.

"I'm glad you're not marrying a cow paddy because you'll never get out of here acting that crazy. I'm getting out of here in a week," Crazy Bob said.

"I want you to me my best man," Potbelly said again.

"Best man for what?" Crazy Bob asked.

"I want you to be my best man at the wedding, you crazy old fool. I love you; you're my oldest friend," Potbelly said.

Crazy Bob started to tear up; he was overwhelmed with emotion.

"I've never been anyone's best man before," Crazy Bob said.

"You're the best man I know, besides Drake, of course, who I will ask to be one of my groomsman; but you and I have been friends longer. We came here at the same time, almost thirty-six years ago," Potbelly said.

"I guess I will have to stop working on expanding so I can fit into my old suit," Crazy Bob said.

"I think we can afford to buy you a new one," Potbelly said.

"Nonsense, I'll just have my wife make one. She is really good with her sewing machine; she can even make a pair of asses," Crazy Bob said.

"That sounds fine, Bob," Potbelly said.

Chapter 47

They were calling it C-Day for Crazy Day. It was just like D-Day except no one stormed any beaches. Crazy Bob did storm the kitchen for a ham sandwich in a blitzkrieg fashion, but no one died that they were aware of.

It was perfect timing because the board was having its quarterly board meeting when it got the news.

Jasmine, Dr. Raven's secretary, poked her head into the board meeting.

"Dr. Raven, there is a very important call you should take," Jasmine said.

"Can't it wait? We are right in the middle of voting on our bonuses," Dr. Raven said.

"No, it's urgent; and the gentleman insists that you put him on the—and I quote—'speaker phone thingy' because he has something to say to the board," Jasmine said.

"Alright, turn the speaker phone on. This better not be one of those crank calls we get annually from that patient of ours—what's his name—Crazy Freddy or Bob or something?" Dr. Raven said.

"Hello there," Drake said into the speaker.

"This is Dr. Raven, as well as the entire board of Looney Bin Incorporated," Dr. Raven said.

"Not anymore; you are no longer on the board of Looney Bin Incorporated," Drake said.

"Who is this? Is this a joke?" Dr. Raven asked.

"This is Drake of Looney Bin Incorporated. I'm just one of the many employees you've been screwing for years. It is a joke; it's the best joke ever played, but it also happens to be true. You have been bought out; you no longer have control over the company," Drake said.

"I don't believe you; we would have noticed if someone was buying up large shares," Dr. Raven said.

Crazy Bob interrupted, "Haven't you ever heard of a not-friendly takeover?"

"You mean a hostile takeover," Drake said.

"Right, I meant hostile," Crazy Bob said.

"We filed a form 13-D with the Securities and Exchange Commission, so you can call them to verify what I am telling you," Drake said.

"Later, bitches," Crazy Bob said.

Drake hung up the phone, and Dr. Raven continued to discuss bonuses.

"Didn't you hear what that man said?" Dr. Yardley asked.

"It's ridiculous; we would know if someone has acquired our company. I mean, wouldn't we?" Dr. Raven asked with a little insecurity in his voice.

No one said anything; for the first time, Dr. Raven didn't sound sure of himself. In that moment Dr. Raven didn't seem like the God they all thought he had been. He was just a man; he was not infallible.

"I don't think we need to call the SEC," Dr. Yardley said.

He showed Dr. Raven the headline on his phone.

Out-Loonied, Looney Bin Incorporated outmaneuvered.

Dr. Raven pounded his fist on the table.

"How in the hell could we not have known about this?" Dr Raven asked.

"It must have been a closely guarded secret," Dr. Sherman said.

Dr. Raven looked up at Dr. Sherman, who glanced away quickly. He tried to make eye contact with the others, but no one would catch his eye as the realization hit him.

"You all knew about this, didn't you?" Dr. Raven asked.

No one replied; they were still a little afraid of him.

"Of course you knew. They came to you with an offer. What were the terms?" Dr Raven asked.

No one spoke for a while until finally Dr. Johnson found his courage.

"Just that we could all remain on the board; only you had to go."

"I see, so that's how it is? You all are jealous of me; you wish you had the balls to do what I do. This company would have never become so profitable without me. I put this company on the map. This company will die without me. You will all die without me too. You will wilt and die."

Dr. Raven spit on the board room table and stormed out.

Dr. Sherman hit the intercom.

"Jasmine, have security escort Dr. Raven out and make sure he is not allowed back in the building."

"Yes, right away," Jasmine said.

It was true that Drake, Crazy Bob and Potbelly, along with Cow Paddy, had approached the other board members. They realized that the root of the cancer was Dr. Raven, and they had to get rid of him at all costs. They needed to make sure he stayed in the dark, and the best way to do that was to make a deal with the others. It was a risk, but one that paid off because as it turned out, they all hated and feared Dr. Raven and wanted nothing more than to see him gone. Some of the older board members didn't like the way the company was being run and the reputation it had in the business community.

"Well, I believe this board meeting is adjourned," Dr. Yardley said.

When Drake hung up the phone with the board, he turned to the group.

"Now we have one more fish to fry."

"I think we are having ham today, not fish," Crazy Bob said.

"No, I mean Dr. Boyd," Drake said.

"We are going to fry Dr. Boyd?" Potbelly asked.

"Not fry, but fire," Drake said.

"I prefer my fish broiled," Crazy Bob said.

"Is Dr. Boyd in his office?" Drake asked.

"Yes, he should be; I'm supposed to have an appointment with him now," Crazy Bob said.

They all marched down the hall to Dr. Boyd's office except for the new patient, Max, who was busy turning the light switch on and off in his room a hundred times. He would have been finished with his routine, but he lost count around eighty-seven and had to start over. He firmly believed that if his morning ritual were not carried out, something very bad would happen.

Crazy Bob walked into the office first.

"You're late, Robert; what's going on here?" Dr. Boyd asked.

"I'm afraid you're the one who is late," Crazy Bob said.

Dr. Boyd had no idea what he was talking about; and neither did Crazy Bob, for that matter.

"Huh?" Dr. Boyd said.

"What my esteemed colleague means is, 'You're fired,'" Drake said.

"Guys, I don't have time for this. Robert and I have are supposed to be having a session right now," Dr. Boyd said.

"We know you got Dr. Olive removed from his position and sent to solitary confinement. You drove him over the edge. You never help anyone; you just want to keep up the company's profits," Drake said.

"That's absurd. You can't fire me; only the board can do that," Dr. Boyd said.

"Well, they have," Drake said.

Drake handed him the deed.

"Crazybook acquired Looney Bin Incorporated in a stock purchase of $51,000 worth of shares," Dr. Boyd read.

"I'm afraid you're out," Drake said.

"This doesn't mean I'm out," Dr. Boyd said.

"Flip the paper over," Potbelly said.

"P.S. You're fired, Dr. Boyd," Dr. Boyd read.

It was written and signed by Dr. Yardley, the new chairman.

"You know what, you're all just a bunch of lunatics; and you're never getting out of here. You're going to die at Looney Bin Incorporated," Dr. Boyd said.

"I'm not going to die here; I know exactly how I'm going to die. I'm going to be crushed to death by a rolling bale of hay, then bludgeoned and castrated and thrown into the Dead Sea," Crazy Bob said.

"Do you mean your body is going to be thrown into the Dead Sea or your penis?" Potbelly asked.

"My penis. I assume my body will be buried here," Crazy Bob said.

"See what I mean? What damn nonsense! I'm sick of it; you're all hopeless," Dr. Boyd said.

He marched out of his office, not bothering to take any of his personal effects. He didn't want anything; he just wanted to leave quickly.

"I wouldn't mind being killed by a rolling hay bale; it would be way more fun than a heart attack," Drake said.

"I can arrange that for you," Crazy Bob said.

"Would you really do that for me?" Drake asked.

"Of course, what are friends for?" Crazy Bob said.

Chapter 48

Today was the day that Potbelly was getting married to Sue. The wedding was to take place there at Looney Bin Incorporated.

Everyone was standing still and holding their breath, waiting for Crazy Bob, the best man, to produce the ring. He patted his pants pockets and reached inside his coat pocket and pulled out a gold ring. There was a collective exhale, but it was premature because Crazy Bob dropped the ring on the floor.

He bent over to pick it up, and the back of his pants split. The ring had rolled underneath Lester's chair. Lester, who had been picking his nose throughout the ceremony, reached underneath his seat with the same hand and retrieved the ring. He gave it to Crazy Bob, who wiped the ring on his shirt and gave it to Potbelly.

"Place the ring on her finger," the priest said.

Nurse Lovington blubbered so loudly throughout the ceremony and kept blowing her nose into a handkerchief that it startled baby Olivia, who was trying to sleep and also began crying. It made it difficult to hear the priest.

Potbelly put the ring on Sue's finger, who smiled a big buck-toothed smile.

Nurse Lovington blew her nose for the umpteenth time.

"You may now kiss the bride," the priest said.

"Did he say, 'You may now have sex with the bride'?" Abram asked.

"I think he said kiss; they have sex later in bed when no one is watching," Lester said.

"That's too bad," Abram said.

"I would like to be wed; I would like to have sex in bed," Sam said.

"Me too, Sam," Lester said.

The reception was also being held in the dayroom. Nurse Lovington hung up the disco ball, the same one that was used at all of Crazy Bob's going-away parties and the same one that Dr. Olive used to hang himself; it was very versatile.

Crazy Bob cut himself a generous portion of cake; even though they had won and were now in control of Looney Bin Incorporated, he still wanted to keep expanding. Crazy Bob was enterprising, after all; and his ambition was to expand more than anyone else had before.

Godot showed up late and missed the whole wedding. They waited for him as long as they could, but the priest said he had another wedding to get to. Virgil showed up with the wax head of Virgil under his arm. He watched the entire wedding from underneath the coffee table.

"Okay, everyone; it's time to give the wedding gift. We gave it a lot of thought, and we all chipped in to get this one gift which we thought was the one thing every newly-married couple needed," Drake said.

Nurse Lovington presented them with a wicker basket, and inside that wicker basket was none other than a baby pot-bellied pig. Potbelly's eyes lit up.

"She's beautiful," Potbelly said.

"That's a weird-looking sex toy," Crazy Bob said.

"It's a *he*, actually," Nurse Lovington said.

Potbelly took him out of the basket. He was brown and had white spots. He hugged it and gave it a little kiss on its sleepy forehead.

"I'm going to call you Big Pig II," he said.

Everyone clapped; Potbelly had finally gotten his pot-bellied pig.

"I have an announcement too; I'm leaving sometime in the near future, so this wedding celebration is also my goodbye party," Crazy Bob said.

Everyone nodded; it was Crazy Bob's 83rd farewell celebration, and they looked forward to his 84th.

A slow song played on the radio, and Potbelly danced with his new bride. He held her close and whispered something in her ear, which made her blush. Nurse Lovington was dancing with Dr. Mannequin Olive, and the baby was in between them strapped to Nurse Lovington's chest. The baby didn't seem to mind being squeezed between both of her parents; Nurse Lovington had finally stopped crying so she was able to go to sleep. Nurse Lovington had her arms around Dr. Mannequin Olive waist, and his feet weren't even touching the ground.

Crazy Bob cut himself another piece of cake. Abram was only interested in the soda and was on his fifth cup. Between him and Crazy Bob, there would soon be nothing left for anyone else.

Everyone was laughing and having a good time until the party crasher arrived.

He was dressed all in black and looked similar to how the gang was dressed when trying to spring Virgil from solitary confinement, only he was wearing a black ski mask as opposed to shoe polish. He had, though, the one thing Crazy Bob couldn't get because he couldn't pass a background check; and that was an AK-47 assault rifle.

"All right, everyone, down on the ground," he yelled.

No one moved; they thought he was supposed to be the entertainment that was hired for the party.

He fired his gun into the ceiling, but still no one moved.

"What the hell is wrong with you people? Are you crazy?" the man in black asked.

"Why yes, as a matter of fact we are; didn't you see the company name on the front door?" Potbelly asked.

"I know you are crazy; but I didn't think you were crazy, crazy," the man in black said.

"Most of us here are crazy, crazy," Drake said.

"I thought I hired a clown," Nurse Lovington said.

The man in black walked over to Nurse Lovington and slipped on some soda that Abram had spilled on the floor. He landed flat on his back and dropped the assault rifle.

Everyone laughed and clapped.

Crazy Bob picked up the assault rifle and examined it.

"I am not a clown!" he yelled.

This only made everyone laugh harder.

"Where are your rubber nose and clown shoes?" Crazy Bob asked.

"I don't have any because I am not a clown. I am here to kidnap you all," the man in black said.

"I'm really busy with my placebo company and now with Looney Bin Incorporated; I don't think I'll have time to be kidnapped," Drake said.

"I'm afraid you caught me on a bad day as well; I'm leaving tomorrow," Crazy Bob said.

"I don't care if it's convenient for you or not," the man in black said.

"You're not really ha-ha funny, are you?" Drake said.

"I'm sorry, Mr. Clown; but my wife and I have to be going. We're on our honeymoon, and we have tickets to Hawaii," Potbelly said.

"I am not a clown, and nobody is going anywhere," the man in black said exasperatedly.

"At least give him a chance to do some tricks," Lester said.

The man in black turned to Crazy Bob.

"Give me back my rifle," he said.

He was about to do that when the real clown stumbled in. His makeup was smeared, his wig was askew and he smelled of liquor and vomit.

"It looks like we have two clowns," Potbelly said.

"I only hired one," Nurse Lovington said.

He belched. Despite his white face paint, he looked positively green.

"Did someone call for a clown?" the clown asked.

"I did," Nurse Lovington said.

"I'm Giggles the Clown."

He reached into his yellow blazer with polka dots to pull out a business card. He handed it to Nurse Lovington.

If you want a giggle, call Giggles the Clown. Available for Birthday parties, Bar mitzvahs and special occasions. Kinky fee $35.00.

"What is a kinky fee?" Nurse Lovington asked.

"If I have to do anything kinky, like tie someone up and whip them or have sex with a midget," Giggles said.

He looked around at the crowd. Abram was on his tenth soda, and he was twitching and hopping around on one leg. Fritz had on his SS uniform, Crazy Bob was still holding the assault rifle, Godot was naked, Nurse Lovington was holding a mannequin and there was a man dressed in black camouflage and a ski mask.

"Looks like I'm going to need that fee upfront," Giggles said.

"We don't have any midgets, but you can tie one of us up and whip us if you want," Crazy Bob said.

"No one is doing anything; you are all coming with me. I am a kidnapper—why can't you people get that through your heads?" the man in black said.

"I have another party to do after this one so I can't be kidnapped," Giggles the Clown said.

He reached into his jacket and pulled out a flask and took a long swallow.

"I don't think you people understand how kidnapping works. I take all of you and hold you for ransom. I don't have to do it at your convenience; you have to do it at my convenience and as it happens, my schedule is free, thanks to all of you. Not you, Mr. Giggles, I'm afraid you're just a victim of circumstance," the man in black said.

"What do you mean, thanks to all of us? I'm beginning to think you're not a clown at all. Crazy Bob, hold on to that assault rifle. Keep it pointed at our new friend," Nurse Lovington said.

Crazy Bob pointed the assault rifle at Giggles the Clown, who was so startled he dropped his flask and raised his hands.

"Please don't shoot. I've got five children and three ex-wives that I have to provide for," Giggles the Clown said.

"Not him, Crazy Bob; point it at the man in black," Nurse Lovington said.

"You want me to point it at Johnny Cash?" Crazy Bob asked, a little aghast.

"He's not Johnny Cash," Nurse Lovington said.

She walked over to the man in black and yanked off his ski mask. There was a collective gasp; it was Dr. Raven.

"I saw this same thing happen on an episode of 'Scooby Doo' once," Potbelly said.

"This always happens on an episode of 'Scooby Doo,'" Drake said.

"On the episode I saw, it wasn't a doctor who was the villain, though; it turned out to be old man Jenkins, the prospector," Potbelly said.

They were interrupted by a retching noise. Giggles the Clown had vomited on the floor. He wiped his mouth with his sleeve.

"Why are you doing this, Dr. Raven?" Nurse Lovington asked.

"You people have ruined my life. I have nothing left. I mean I still have billions of dollars, my health, my family and three vacation homes; but what good is all of that if I don't have the company my grandfather founded. You've taken away my dignity, my self-esteem and my manhood; you've castrated me," Dr. Raven said.

"Ve cut off your viener?" Fritz asked.

Godot, who was naked, involuntarily grabbed his wiener as if he were going to be next.

"Yes, metaphorically speaking," Dr. Raven said.

"Sam, call the police," Nurse Lovington said.

Sam, who was closest to the phone, picked it up and dialed 911.

"911, what is your emergency?" the operator asked.

"It is me. We have an emergency," Sam said.

"What is your name?" The operator asked.

"I am Sam. Sam I am," Sam said.

"Okay, this line if for emergencies only," the operator said.

"We need to run; he's got a gun," Sam said.

"I don't have a gun anymore; you have the gun," Dr. Raven said.

"Are you being held against your will?" the operator asked.

"We all agree; we want to be free," Sam said.

"Sir, this line is for emergencies only. If you don't have an emergency, you need to hang up the phone," the operator said.

Sam was sweaty and getting frazzled. He was trying to think of what to say to her; but before he could, the cops arrived.

It was a SWAT team, and they kicked in the door. Someone must have already called them when they heard the gunshots.

"Everyone, down on the floor!"

Everyone got down on the floor, and Crazy Bob was still holding on to the gun. The SWAT team swarmed him.

"Drop the weapon!"

Crazy Bob looked up and saw the SWAT team with their weapons all pointed at him.

"Are you talking to me?" Crazy Bob asked.

"Yes, drop it."

Crazy Bob laid down the weapon, and one of the SWAT guys picked it up.

They handcuffed everyone, including baby Olivia Olive, who was still sleeping.

"I'm afraid I have to respectively decline to be arrested; I have another party to go to," Giggles the Clown said.

"You will have to come with us until this matter is resolved," A SWAT team member said.

One of the guys on the SWAT team was having trouble getting Dr. Mannequin Olive's arms behind him to handcuff him.

"Sergeant, this guy doesn't seem to want to cooperate."

The sergeant, who was a giant of a man, took his baton off his belt and hit Dr. Mannequin Olive in the face with it. Dr. Mannequin Olive didn't budge.

Nurse Lovington screamed.

"Don't you touch my husband!"

"Oh, a tough guy," the sergeant said.

The sergeant took out his taser and used it on Dr. Mannequin

Olive.

Dr. Mannequin Olive didn't budge; he just stared at the sergeant. The sergeant stared back, trying to figure out what to do with him next when all of a sudden, there was a pungent stench. There was smoke coming from Dr. Mannequin Olive. The taser had melted some of his plastic.

The sergeant took a closer look at him and removed his wig.

"This is a mannequin," he said.

"You brute, what have you done to my husband?" Nurse Lovington asked.

"You're married to a mannequin? Lady, you are one sick puppy," the sergeant said.

"Who are you to judge?" Nurse Lovington asked.

One of the other SWAT team members, a rookie, was trying to put handcuffs on Godot; but his arm fell off.

"Looks like this one is a mannequin too, Sergeant," the rookie said.

"I am not a mannequin," Godot said.

"Holy shit, Sarge; this one talks," the rookie said.

"This place really is a looney bin. Alright, leave him here. I'm not dragging any mannequins back to the station," the Sergeant said.

"I am not a mannequin," Godot protested again.

"Shut up, or I'll give you the same treatment I gave your friend," the sergeant said.

The rest of the SWAT team swept the building, making sure there was no one else hiding out. Finally, when they felt like the building was secure, they evacuated everyone and piled them into the police vans they had outside. There was no one in the building left except a burnt Dr. Mannequin Olive, who was lying on the floor, still smoking, and a naked Godot.

Godot looked around and scratched himself. He propped Dr. Mannequin Olive in a chair and sat down beside him.

"I am not a mannequin," he said sheepishly.

Chapter 49

After several hours of questioning, everyone was let go except for Dr. Raven, who would be facing breaking and entering charges as well as attempted kidnapping. Also, Giggles the Clown was detained because there was a warrant out for his arrest. He was delinquent in his child support payments.

Dr. Mannequin Olive, Nurse Lovington and Olivia went back home. Potbelly, along with his new bride and Big Pig II, their pot-bellied pig, went with them. Potbelly was going to work at Insane in the Brain Incorporated, while Sue was going to stay at home because they wanted to start a family right away. They wanted at least ten kids; and Potbelly wanted to name them all Crazy Bob and Drake, even if some were girls, after his two dearest friends.

Looney Bin Incorporated was thriving. The corporate waste and greed were gone, and it was replaced with a fellowship of fraternity and love for the common man. Drake was appointed CEO, and his placebo company became a very profitable division of Looney Bin Inc. Drake only wished that his grandparents were still alive and could see that their trip to the new country, as they always called it, had paid off for one of their descendants.

Abram, Lester, Sam, Fritz and the new patient, Max, all stayed on and continued working for Looney Bin Incorporated, each one finally receiving a wage. Fritz had to attend a diversity course, where he received extensive training in culture and diversity. He came back a new man, one that wasn't anti-Semitic.

In addition to being given a wage, they were each given company cars; and Abram was given an unlimited amount of free soda. He no longer had dissociative boredom disorder, because he was kept so busy. Sam was busy too; he enjoyed answering the phone. "Come on out and don't be lazy, if you know you're really crazy. This is Sam. Sam I am."

Virgil continued to write the great American novel, and he was quite successful at it. He met up with Margaret, the girl whose Play-Doh face he had urinated on in school. He made another face for her out of wax and presented it to her. As it turned out, she still had a crush on him; and they decided to get married.

There would be no more waiting for Godot; he finally died from the leprosy. He was two days late to his own funeral. His insides just decided to stop working. He lay in the casket in his top hat and underwear. Crazy Bob took the top hat off of his head and told everyone that Godot had bequeathed him the hat. The new patient, Max, was in charge of filling out and filing the forms. With his OCD, he was the perfect candidate because he was very meticulous with every *i* dotted and every *t* crossed. They originally had him answering the phones, but he had to wait for the telephone to ring 100 times before he could answer it, so they decided that wasn't good for business. Most people hung up after the first ten rings.

Drake walked into the dayroom which had been converted into offices.

"Has anyone seen Crazy Bob? I wanted to talk to him about an idea I had," Drake said.

"No, no one has seen him today; I think the Canadians might have kidnapped him," Lester said.

Lester still told lies and still believed the Canadians were plotting to overthrow the United States. They were just sitting up there behind their wholesome façade of maple syrup and hand-knitted scarves, waiting for the opportunity to strike.

"Maybe the stink bugs in his head drove him mad," Abram said.

"He was already mad. Guys, this is serious; where is Crazy Bob?" Drake asked.

"I think maybe he finally left," Lester said.

It was true; Crazy Bob was gone. He had finally left Looney Bin Incorporated. He had said he was leaving at Potbelly and Sue's wedding, but no one had paid any attention because he always said he was leaving and never had. He was the Crazy Bob who cried wolf. In retrospect, Drake thought his friend seemed sad on what should have been a joyous day. He probably was a little disappointed that no one was making a big deal of his leaving.

Of course, if they had known he was leaving for sure this time, they would have made a great big deal of it. They would have pleaded with him to stay; and if he couldn't be talked out of it, then at least they would have given him going-away presents.

There was a lot of speculation as to where he went. Lester worried that the stink bugs inside his head had taken over and driven him to kill. Drake thought he might have gone back to teaching; but after contacting every university where Crazy Bob had claimed he taught, he came up with nothing. Fritz theorized that he had joined the Aryan nation and became a neo-Nazi skinhead. Abram suggested that he might have gone back to live with some of his relatives in the town that he was from; but no one knew any of his relatives to contact because in thirty-five years at Looney Bin Incorporated, no one had ever come to see Crazy Bob. He wasn't with Potbelly and Sue or working at Insane in the Brain Corporation.

Months went by, and they had not heard anything from their dear friend, until one day out of the blue, a post card arrived. Drake gathered everyone in the dayroom; Potbelly was also there visiting. The post card was a picture of Crazy Bob with a group of pygmies. The pygmies were naked except for a loin cloth, and Crazy Bob was wearing a Bermuda shirt and khaki shorts. He was giving the thumbs-up sign.

Greetings from Uganda; I joined the Peace Corp and was assigned the tribe of pygmies that Potbelly once helped. P.B., you will be happy to know that they don't eat pot-bellied pigs anymore; they are now vegetarians. I'm enjoying my new life, but I miss all of you very much. You're always in my heart. I love you guys and remember, "We shall meet in the place where there is no darkness."
Love,
Crazy Bob.

"I'm glad to hear that those pygmies stopped eating pot-bellied pigs," Potbelly said.

"He looks happy," Lester said.

"What does that last line mean? What is the place where there is no darkness?" Abram asked.

"Duz he mean zum place zunny?" Fritz asked.

"No, even in sunny places, it still gets dark," Lester said.

"What does it mean?" Potbelly asked.

Drake looked over the post card again and crammed at the very bottom was a post script.

P.S. It's a metaphor.

Drake took the post card and walked over to the bulletin board, which was filled with all of Crazy Bob's going-away parties. He pinned the post card beside his last party, which was actually Potbelly and Sue's wedding. Crazy Bob was eating a piece of wedding cake. He was holding the cake in one hand and giving the thumbs-up sign with the other, as he did in all of his photographs.

It was a metaphor, so it now made perfect sense; they knew where they had to go to meet Crazy Bob.